without
a Trace

Patricia H. Rushford

Jennie McGrady Mystery Series

1. Too Many Secrets
2. Silent Witness
3. Pursued
4. Deceived
5. Without a Trace

Without a Trace

Patricia H. Rushford

BETHANY HOUSE PUBLISHERS
MINNEAPOLIS, MINNESOTA 55438

Without a Trace
Patricia Rushford

Cover illustration by Andrea Jorgenson

Library of Congress Catalog Card Number 95–7454

ISBN 1–55661–558–2

Copyright © 1995
Patricia Rushford

Published by Bethany House Publishers
A Ministry of Bethany Fellowship, Inc.
11300 Hampshire Avenue South
Minneapolis, Minnesota 55438

Printed in the United States of America

To Christopher and Corisa,
my grandchildren and
my greatest fans.

PATRICIA RUSHFORD is an award-winning writer, speaker, and teacher who has published almost twenty books and numerous articles, including *What Kids Need Most in a Mom, The Humpty Dumpty Syndrome: Putting Yourself Back Together Again*, and her first young adult novel, *Kristen's Choice*. She is a registered nurse and has a master's degree in counseling from Western Evangelical Seminary. She and her husband, Ron, live in Washington State and have two grown children, six grandchildren, and lots of nephews and nieces.

Pat has been reading mysteries for as long as she can remember and is delighted to be writing a series of her own. She is a member of Mystery Writers of America, Society of Children's Book Writers and Illustrators, and several other writing organizations. She is also co-director of writer's weekend at the Beach.

1

"Mom?" Jennie McGrady set her suitcase in the dark entry, flipped on the light switch, and closed the door. Her long dark braid swung forward, then back again as she straightened. "Mom!" she yelled again, this time leaning against the banister and directing her voice up the stairs. "I'm home. Why didn't you pick me up at the airport?"

She braced herself for the welcome-home cheers and the little five-year-old brother who would appear at any moment, leap into her arms, and give her one of his super-duper bear hugs. Nick didn't come. The unexpected silence wrapped an ominous web around her. Both cars were in the driveway. They should be home.

Jennie raced up the stairs two at a time. She stopped at her bedroom first, wondering if they were waiting there to surprise her, but found no one to greet her except the dozens of stuffed animals she'd collected over the years.

She made her way down the hall, poked her head into Nick's room, then Mom's. Their beds hadn't been slept in. Hurrying back down the stairs she called again. "Mom? Nick?" Her pulse quickened. She scanned the living room. Two glass eyes peered at her from the couch. Jennie scooped up Coco, Nick's favorite stuffed bear, and hugged him.

"Come on, you two. You can come out now." When no one answered, she tightened her hold on Coco and hurried past the dining area into the kitchen hoping for a note that would explain their absence. She flipped on the switch and the room exploded with white light from the recessed florescent fixtures in the ceiling.

No note. The spotless white counter and sink reminded her of a movie she'd seen once where all the residents of a small midwestern town disappeared. She couldn't remember why.

Jennie set Coco down, bolted to the fridge and threw open the door, almost laughing with relief when she saw the leftover milk in Nick's Mickey Mouse glass. A piece of fried chicken with one small bite taken out sat next to it.

Leaning into the refrigerator, she shook her head and eyed its contents for something to drink. *You really are something, McGrady. Getting spooked over an empty house like a little kid. You're sixteen, for Pete's sake.* Jennie had come home to an empty house before, of course, but this seemed different. Okay, maybe Mom and Nick had gone shopping and were late getting back. Or maybe Michael, Mom's sort-of boyfriend, had taken them to a movie or to the park, or for a ride up the Columbia River Gorge. There were a million explanations. So why didn't any of them sound right?

Because Mom would never forget you. The voice hung in the air as if someone had spoken it. Jennie frowned, remembering how disappointed she'd been when

Mom and Nick weren't at the airport to meet her plane. Jennie and Lisa Calhoun, her cousin and best friend, had just returned from a cruise in the Caribbean with Gram and her new husband, J.B. Mom should have been there. Instead, she had called Aunt Kate, Dad's twin sister, asking her to pick Jennie up at the airport and drop her off at the house.

"She didn't say why," Kate had said when Jennie asked. "She just said something had come up."

Jennie shoved aside the growing apprehension by telling herself that if it were anything serious, Mom would have told Aunt Kate. Being sisters-in-law, they usually told each other everything.

Jennie scanned the refrigerator shelves, then reached behind the milk carton to grab a diet cola and smiled at Mom's not-so-subtle reminder. Mom always put the Coke behind the milk as a subtle reminder that milk was the preferred drink. She started to pop back the top of the can, then changed her mind and pulled out the milk instead.

When she opened the cupboard to retrieve a glass, the back door opened. "Are you sure you checked the entire house?" a man's voice said. Jennie recognized it. Michael Rhodes, Mom's boyfriend. Or at least he had been. They'd gotten engaged a few weeks ago. Then Mom started having second thoughts. *"Michael is too much like your father,"* Mom had said. She was wrong, of course. Mom had been wrong about a lot of things lately.

Michael was nothing like Dad. Jason McGrady worked as an undercover agent for the Drug Enforcement Administration, the DEA. Michael built houses and planned to become a minister.

At first Jennie had resented Michael. Now she wasn't sure how she felt. She would have preferred to have Dad come back home, but like he'd said, "You can't have everything the way you want it." Jennie shook off the memories and the confusion that accompanied them when she thought about the circumstances surrounding her mom and dad and focused her attention on Mom and Michael.

Mom walked into the kitchen, with Michael only a step behind. "I've looked everywhere. The police are out patrolling the neighborhood now. I can't imagine—" she stopped in midsentence and stared at Jennie. "Oh, Baby," Mom cried as she closed the distance between them and wrapped her arms around Jennie's waist. "I'm so glad you're back."

With Mom being nearly a head shorter than Jennie, hugging still felt awkward. For a moment she rested her chin on Mom's auburn hair, feeling more like the mother than the daughter. When Mom drew back there were tears in her eyes. "I'm so sorry I couldn't be at the airport. I . . ." She glanced back at Michael as if she expected him to finish her sentence. He didn't.

"Hi, Jennie." He sounded as though he were addressing someone at a funeral. He closed the door and leaned against it. "Welcome back." Turning to Mom he said, "I'll check with the police again—find out what I can do to help. Unless you want me to be here when you tell her."

"No." Mom took a deep breath and sighed. "Thanks. I'll take care of it."

"What's wrong?" Jennie's stomach tightened. It didn't take a mind reader to know why Mom was so upset. "It's Nick, isn't it? Something has happened to Nick."

2

Mom pinched her lips together and nodded. "He's gone. We can't find him anywhere. We've called the police."

Jennie felt like she'd been slugged in the stomach. She leaned against the counter for support. Along with Mom and Dad, Nick was the most important person in her life. "You think he's been kidnapped?"

Mom shook her head. "It's more likely he ran away." She reached into her pocket, dragged out a balled-up tissue, and blew her nose. "It's my fault. I should have realized how attached he'd become to Michael. I thought maybe the dog would help."

"What dog? What are you talking about?" Jennie fought against the growing hysteria. She refused to let herself think about what might happen to a little boy alone on the streets at night and concentrated instead on what Mom was saying.

"Michael and I . . ." Mom paused to grab a fresh tissue from the box near the telephone, then continued. "Two days ago I broke up with Michael. I realized I couldn't let things go on. Nick was getting too attached to him and I thought it would be better if we

11

just didn't see each other for a while." Mom wobbled as though she were about to collapse.

"Maybe you'd better sit down." Jennie put an arm around her shoulder and pulled a chair away from the kitchen table. Mom sank into it and offered Jennie a teary thank-you. Jennie dropped into the chair next to her.

"Anyway, Nick didn't take it well. I've never seen him so upset. Michael and I tried to explain things to him. How do you say something like that to a child?"

Jennie didn't answer. She wished someone could explain Mom's rationale to her. Jennie had solved a number of mysteries lately, but trying to figure Mom out topped them all. Again Jennie drew her attention back to Nick. "You said something about a dog. What's that all about?"

"I thought maybe Nick would take the news about Michael better if we got him a dog. You know how he's been wanting one. Ever since he saw that movie *Beethoven*." Mom stopped to blow her nose. "So I got him one. Michael came along to help pick him out. Bernie—that's what Nick named him—is a St. Bernard puppy."

"You think Nick ran away?"

"This afternoon Nick asked if he could go visit Michael. When I said no, he threw a fit. He finally settled down, and I thought we'd gotten through the worst of it. But later, when I called him in to get ready to go to the airport, he was gone. I called Kate and asked her to pick you up. I didn't want to worry anyone. You know how he likes to hide. Anyway, I thought he was here. I searched the house, and when I couldn't find him I called Michael and notified the police. We checked the neighborhood and I called Kate back, but they'd already left for the airport. I left a message on their machine that Nick is missing."

Jennie had no idea what to do with the emotions churning around inside her. She bounced to her feet and started pacing. Part of her wanted to attack Mom. *What kind of mother are you? How could you lose Nick?* Another part hoped it was all just a bad dream.

While Jennie was sorting through it all, the back door flew open. Aunt Kate came in first, then Uncle Kevin, who was Mom's brother and Kate's husband. A few seconds later Lisa and Kurt, Lisa's little brother, Gram and J.B. appeared. Jennie watched them as though she were somewhere outside of herself, seeing a made-for-television movie.

"We left the minute we got your message. Have you found him?" Gram asked, giving Mom and then Jennie a hug.

Mom shook her head and dabbed the corner of her eyes with a tissue.

"What happened and what can we do to help?" Kate opened a cupboard and took down coffee fixings.

Mom repeated the same story she'd told Jennie. "I wish I could be out there looking for him, but the police officer said I should stay here—in case Nick comes home or someone calls."

"You must be frantic." Kate poured water into the coffee maker and switched it on.

Mom closed her eyes and rolled her head back as Gram massaged her shoulders. "I'm trying not to be."

"I'm certain they'll find him, Susan," Gram reassured. "Nine times out of ten these things turn out to be false alarms. Most missing children usually turn up at their house or at a neighbor's."

"I hope that's the case." Kate took down four cups from the wooden mug rack on the wall. "What about flyers? Shouldn't we be making up flyers? Alert the media?"

"It's a bit too soon for that, lass," J.B. said.

Gram glanced at J.B. and kept massaging Mom's neck. For a second Jennie thought Gram would argue with him and was strangely disappointed when she didn't. "J.B.'s right. The police will probably want to do a complete search of the neighborhood first."

Jennie was still trying to adjust to Gram and J.B.'s recent marriage. It seemed strange to think about a grandparent falling in love. *What's really strange, McGrady, is that you're thinking about them when you should be concentrating on finding Nick.*

"Still, it wouldn't hurt to have a flyer ready," Kate insisted. "It will give us something constructive to do."

Constructive. Jennie took a deep breath and released her grip on the chair. She hadn't even realized she'd been holding on to it.

"Aren't we gonna go look for Nick?" Kurt asked, echoing Jennie's thoughts. It seemed to her they were wasting valuable time talking when they could be out looking. If Nick really was missing, they needed to act quickly.

Gram wrapped an arm around Kurt's shoulders and pulled him close. A flicker of pain passed over her features. "Yes, we certainly are. But we need to work with the police. It won't do Nick a bit of good if we go off helter-skelter. We need a plan."

Like Kurt, Jennie wanted to get moving. But Gram was probably right. The first part of Gram's plan would be to pray. It always was. Before Gram even suggested it, they all closed their eyes hoping that God would keep Nick safe and that they would find him soon. Jennie also prayed for strength for herself. She already felt fragmented, her thoughts scattered, confused.

A police officer came in with Michael just as Gram uttered a final amen. "I wish I could say your prayers have been answered, Helen." He nodded toward Gram, then reached out and shook her hand. "Nice to see you again."

Gram introduced him as Robert Beck. She'd worked with him before leaving the Portland Police Department ten years before.

"Sorry about your grandson," Beck said. "I've been through the house and checked with the neighbors. I just patrolled the area by car. Didn't see any sign of Nick or the dog. The good news is that we haven't seen anything that might indicate foul play. Just to be on the safe side, though, I've reported the case to my supervisor. He's alerted the other officers so they'll also be on the lookout for him."

"What can we do to help?" Gram asked.

"I'll need a list of all his playmates and neighbors he talks to. You folks might want to work the neighborhood again, while we expand the perimeter by car. The more people we have out looking, the better our chances."

"Why don't Lisa and I take the area between our house and the end of the block where the Stuarts live?" Jennie suggested. "We pretty much know Nick's play areas. We'll check under the porches, get into the bushes. Nick loves to crawl into places like that."

Officer Beck agreed, then turned back to Mom. "Like I said before, Mrs. McGrady, I'd like you to stay here." To all of them he said, "When you locate him, report back to the house immediately and call the dispatcher."

He'd said *when*, not *if*. When. Jennie clung to the word and wrapped it around her like a lifeline.

The others had gone by the time Jennie could scrounge up two useable flashlights and meet Lisa in the backyard. She handed one to Lisa. "Let's go."

"I want to help too." Kurt jogged along with them. "I need a flashlight."

"You're too young," Lisa said. "Why don't you go help Mom and Aunt Susan?"

"Am not—I'm eleven." Kurt was small for his age and looked more like a third grader than a fifth grader. His chestnut hair and freckles didn't help. Even though he was older than Nick by six years, he always treated Nick like a good buddy.

"Let him come, Lisa. He probably knows Nick's hideouts better than we do. And he can squeeze into the smaller places."

Lisa handed him the flashlight. "Okay, but you need to stay with us."

For the next half hour Jennie and her cousins pointed their flashlight beams into trees and under bushes, under the porch and every possible play area and hiding place. As the search continued, Jennie's hopes faded. Though she tried to stop them, unwanted images from newscasts she'd seen and articles she'd read about missing children crept into her mind. She chased them away and kept looking. Nick had to be close-by—and safe. He just had to be.

After going over every inch of their yard and the neighboring yards, Jennie and Lisa returned to the house. Jennie sank onto the top porch step. Lisa joined her, propped her arms on her knees and rested her head on them. "Got any other ideas?"

"Maybe the others will find something," Jennie said hopefully. She glanced around in a panic. "Where is Kurt?"

Lisa shook her head, her coppery red curls aflame in the warm glow from the porch light. "Relax. He's fine. I sent him in about half an hour ago, remember? He was exhausted and Mom told him to camp out in Nick's room."

She vaguely remembered Lisa and Kurt leaving for a while, but it hadn't registered. Jennie drew in a deep breath to keep her tears at bay.

"You okay?" Lisa straightened and placed a hand on Jennie's arm.

"Not really." Jennie scrambled to her feet and paced from one end of the porch to the other. She passed the porch swing, remembering the dozens of times she and Nick had sat together reading story after story. "I can't imagine Nick running away. He knew I was coming home today."

"And he's nuts about you. He'd have to be really upset to leave home."

"Right. I know he loves Michael, but he loves me too. Nick is around here somewhere. I can feel it."

"But we've looked everywhere. So have the police."

"Maybe we're missing something." Jennie lowered her lanky body into the swing, waited for Lisa to climb in, then set it into motion. Jennie lifted her hair from the back of her neck. During their search most of her braid had come loose. She took out the band, used her fingers to comb through her thick tresses, and fastened it together at the nape of her neck. "To find a kid, you've got to think like a kid. If you were Nick and you were really upset and wanted to get away from your mom for a while, where would you go?"

Lisa shrugged. "When I was little and I got mad at Mom or Dad, I used to go to my room and hide under my bed. Kurt goes out to that big tree in the field behind our house."

"We checked all the beds and trees. Besides, Nick's not into climbing trees—he's into secret places. . . ." Jennie thumped her forehead. "Secret places. That's it! I think I know where he might be."

As they raced into the house and headed up the stairs, Jennie explained. "A year ago Nick and I watched *The Secret Garden* on television."

"I remember seeing that. Some kids found an overgrown garden behind a locked wall and fixed it up."

"Right. I'd forgotten all about it, but at the time, Nick asked me to help him find a secret place of his own. It wasn't hard to do. This house has all kinds of neat little hiding places. Mom knows about most of them, but I don't think she ever found out about this one. Because of the way the roof is shaped, I figured there had to be a crawl space behind Nick's closet. We moved a piece of paneling and sure enough—there was an opening. It's where the roof slopes at the back of the house. I helped him fix it up and he played in it for a while, then seemed to lose interest."

Jennie's hopes accelerated as she entered Nick's room. She turned on the lights, then remembered Kurt was sleeping there. He moaned, covered his eyes, and

18

sat up, his reddish brown hair sticking out at all angles. "Did you find him?"

"Not yet," Lisa answered, "but Jennie thinks he might be in here."

Kurt scrambled out of bed and joined Jennie and Lisa in the closet. Jennie hunkered down and pulled at the miniature door. She felt like the oversized Alice in Wonderland as she got down on her hands and knees and crawled through the small opening. Once her head and shoulders cleared, Jennie paused, afraid he wouldn't be there. Then she swallowed hard and switched on the flashlight.

3

All the frustration, worry, and anxiety that had built up since she'd arrived at the airport swooshed out of her in a huge sigh. "He's here. Go get Mom and the others."

Jennie crawled the rest of the way in. Nick's secret place angled from four feet in height to nothing where the roof met the siding. It was about five feet deep and cluttered with dozens of toys, books, and other treasures she and Mom thought he'd lost. Jennie may have forgotten about Nick's secret place, but Nick certainly hadn't.

In the farthest corner, a familiar five-year-old lump lay cuddled up in his favorite blanket. Beside him was a brown and white lump half Nick's size. As the light flickered over the dog, he raised one eyebrow and peered at her. Then he twitched a little, raised up on his front paws and barked—no, the sound was too deep and resonant for that. He woofed.

"You must be Bernie." Jennie scrunched around into a sitting position. He got up on all fours and woofed again. "Take it easy, big guy," she crooned. "I'm Nick's sister."

The dog moved between her and Nick. One thing

for sure, he took his duties as guard dog seriously. If Nick had run away, Bernie would have done his best to keep him safe.

"What's going on, Bernie?" Nick sat up and rubbed his eyes. "What're you barking at?"

"Hey, Nick, is this any way to greet your big sister? I thought you were going to meet me at the airport."

"Jennie!" Nick scrambled out of his corner and torpedoed into her arms, nearly knocking her over. Bernie hung back for a moment, then greeted her with slobbery licks.

Footsteps sounded on the stairs. Jennie drew him closer and planted a kiss on his head. "I hate to tell you this, little guy, but I think you're going to be in big trouble. How come you went into hiding?"

"Mommy said Michael couldn't be my daddy. But he is. 'Member at my birthday party when God gived him to me?"

Jennie sighed. "I remember, but things don't always turn out the way we'd like them to, Nick. God might still bring you a daddy, it just might not be Michael."

"Are you sure?" Mom asked as she and the others descended on Nick's bedroom. "Where are they?"

"Back here, in the closet," Kurt and Lisa said together.

Nick looked at Jennie accusingly. "You told 'em about my secret place."

"Had to, Nick. Sorry. Maybe we can find you another one."

"Nicholas Jason McGrady," Mom said, poking her head through the opening. "What do you think you're doing, frightening us like that? We've been worried sick about you."

"You'd better hustle on out of here," Jennie whispered in Nick's ear.

Nick disappeared through the hole and landed in his mother's arms. After Aunt Kate, Lisa, Kurt, Michael, Uncle Kevin, J.B. and Gram took turns hugging Nick and telling him how thankful they were that he was okay, Mom asked everyone to go downstairs so she could put Nick to bed. Jennie gave him a final hug and good-night kiss.

By the time Jennie entered the kitchen, Kate had already poured coffee and set a teakettle on to boil. Gram had called the police with the good news.

A few minutes later, Officer Beck returned to the house. Mom apologized to Beck for taking up so much of his time. He didn't seem the least bit annoyed, saying he'd call it even for a cup of coffee.

By midnight everyone had gone home except Michael. Jennie waved goodbye to Gram and J.B. and headed toward the kitchen. "You don't have to help with these," Mom was saying to Michael. Jennie leaned against the doorjamb trying to decide whether to go or stay.

"I know." Michael set the cups and glasses he'd cleared from the table next to the sink, then leaned against the counter. He folded his arms and crossed one leg over the other.

Mom dropped the dishes into the sink and continued washing without looking at him.

Jennie shifted her weight from one foot to the other. She should leave.

"I appreciated your help today," Mom said.

"You don't have to thank me. I love Nick." He loved Mom too, Jennie thought. It seemed strange watching them now. Not long ago she'd hated the idea of Mom marrying Michael and had been relieved when Mom had decided to cool things. Since talking with her father, Jennie's position had shifted. She found herself rooting for Michael. *Come on Mom,* she wanted to say. *Michael's one of the good guys.*

"Nothing's changed between us." Mom wrung out the dishcloth, turned from the sink, and began washing off the table.

Michael's shoulders lifted in a sigh. "Susan . . ."

Whatever he was going to say was lost when Mom interrupted. "How long have you been standing there?"

It took Jennie a few seconds to realize her mother had directed the question at her. Michael's gaze drifted from Susan to Jennie then back again. He looked tired and sad. Jennie felt sorry for him.

"Um . . ." Jennie stammered. "Not long." She pushed off from the wall and walked toward her mother. "Why, am I interrupting a romantic interlude?" Jennie had no idea why she'd said that, or why she'd sounded so sarcastic.

"I'd better get going." Michael moved away from the counter and raised his arms as though he intended to put them around Mom, then lowered them again.

When Mom didn't say anything, Jennie did. "I'll walk you out."

Jennie followed him to the front door. He stepped outside, then turned around to face her. "Well, I guess it's over." His mouth curved in a half-smile. "Remember the day I first came to the house? I stood right here, introduced myself to you, and you ran into the bathroom and threw up."

"You knew? I can't believe Mom told you."

"Susan told me everything—then."

"I was pretty upset with Mom for keeping her relationship with you a secret. I didn't like you much." Jennie paused and, not wanting to meet his eyes, stared at his scuffed white tennis shoes. "Now I'm upset because she's dumping you. Go figure." Jennie raised her head and offered him her hand. "Truce?"

Michael grasped it. "Truce." His grip was warm and firm.

"Maybe Mom will change her mind."

"I doubt it, Jennie. She's made her position pretty clear. But I'm not giving up, not yet anyway. I want you to know that regardless of what happens between your mother and me, I've come to love you and Nick like you were my own kids. If you ever need anything . . ." Unshed tears glistened in his eyes. "Well, you know where you can find me."

Jennie watched until he'd backed his car out of the driveway and driven out of sight. She'd miss driving his BMW. She'd miss him. Jennie shook her head and went back into the house. Mom had to be nuts to send Michael away.

When Jennie got back to the kitchen, her mother had two cups of herbal tea on the table. Mom looked up and smiled. "I know it's late, but I was hoping you'd join me for a cup. I don't know about you, but I've got to wind down a bit. It's been quite a day."

"Sure." Funny how a person could go from being mad at someone one minute, then turn around and feel sorry for them the next. That was how Jennie felt at that moment as she watched her mother lower her slightly overweight body into the chair. Mom looked exhausted. Older, Jennie thought, as though she had too many worries and too little time. It probably didn't help to have a daughter who attracted trouble like a magnet.

After taking a sip of tea, Mom set the cup back on the table. "You didn't have much of a homecoming. I'm sorry we couldn't meet the plane."

Jennie shrugged. "It's okay," she said, warming her hands on the rose-colored mug. "I'm just glad Nick is safe."

"Yes." Mom combed her fingers through auburn bangs, pushing them off her forehead. "Which reminds me, how did you know where to find him?"

Jennie told her how she'd helped Nick find his secret place.

"I'm not sure having secret places is a good idea." Mom paused. "Well, I'm just glad you're home. We can get back to normal again." She pinched her lips together as if she were about to broach a difficult subject. "I don't blame you in any way, Jennie, but I think one of the reasons Nick got so attached to Michael is because you've been gone so much lately."

Jennie braced herself for an argument, then backed down. Mom was right. Jennie had been home only a few days since summer break had started. She and Nick had rarely been separated for more than a weekend before that. No wonder the little guy had been so upset.

"Don't worry, Mom. I'm done traveling for a while. Unless you still want me to go to that counseling camp. I know I said I'd go, but . . ." When Mom first started going out with Michael, Jennie had not taken it well—especially Mom's decision to divorce Dad. Mom's solution had been to send her to a counselor, Gloria, who recommended Jennie attend a camp that helped kids deal with their grief.

"No. That won't be necessary. Gloria and I talked about it and decided you were adjusting quite well." Mom tipped her head and gave her a crooked smile. "Besides, I don't think I want you out of my sight for a while. I about had a heart attack when Gram called me from the cruise ship to tell me you'd been taken captive by that drug lord. One of the reasons I hated your father's work was that I never knew from one day to the next whether he'd survive. Now you seem bent on following in his footsteps."

Jennie winced, wondering what Mom would think if she knew the entire story. "You worry too much. There's probably more chance of my getting killed in a car accident than being killed in the line of duty. Look at Gram and J.B."

Mom sighed. "I can see I'm not going to change your mind. But do me a favor."

"What?"

"At least *try* to stay out of trouble?"

Jennie agreed. It felt good—sitting at the kitchen table with Mom—drinking peppermint tea and talking without fighting. Jennie wondered how long it would last.

"Mom?" Jennie sipped her tea, not sure how to broach the subject. "I know it's none of my business, but why did you break up with Michael? I mean, you said you loved him and now . . ."

"I do love him, Jennie. At least I thought I did. But he's so involved with his work. You know how I feel about that. Going to school, interning at the church, and then working on his contracting job doesn't leave much room for a family."

"What does Michael say about it?"

"Have you been talking to Gloria? She asked me the same thing."

"And. . . ?" Jennie prodded.

"And I haven't mentioned it to him. I can't ask him to give up any of those things. He wants to be a pastor. Without his contracting he wouldn't be able to go to school."

"Why would he have to give them up? Why can't you just work things out like we do? You have a job and I have to go to school. Between us we manage to take care of Nick and the house."

"It sounds like you want me to marry Michael. I thought you hated the idea."

"I did. Now I think maybe you . . . I mean Nick really loves the guy. You should have heard him on his birthday when Michael came. He told me he'd been praying for a daddy and God sent him Michael." The words sounded strange coming from her. Even as she said them, Jennie knew she'd never give up the hope that their real father would come home someday. Of course that was something she could never tell her mother. As far as Mom was concerned, Dad had died in a plane crash five years earlier. Only Jennie and a few people Dad worked with knew otherwise.

"Oh, Jennie," Mom said, a frown creasing her forehead. "That's the hardest part of all this. I didn't want Nick to get hurt. I'm afraid I haven't been completely honest with you and Michael—or myself for that matter. Remember how I said Michael was too much like your father and that's why I backed off?"

Jennie nodded. She didn't agree with Mom's assessment, but decided not to argue.

"While I was in session with Gloria last week, she

said something that made me realize I wasn't anywhere near ready to marry Michael. She called me a hypocrite."

"Why?"

"You know how I was so upset with you because you kept holding on to the hope that your father was alive?"

"You mean you think so too?" For a moment Jennie wondered if Mom knew more than she'd let on.

"No. He's been declared dead, you know that. But I think I was so hard on you because of what I was feeling and didn't want to admit. I still love your father. I wasn't ready to let go either. We had some differences, but I realize now that I can't even think about marrying Michael until . . . I don't know when. I need time to sort through it all. Anyway, I wanted to tell you how sorry I am for trying to hurry you through the grief of losing your dad."

"I'm okay with it now." Jennie wished she could tell her mother the truth about her father's disappearance—and about what really happened on the Caribbean cruise. She'd promised not to, and besides it wouldn't do any good. Dad wouldn't be coming back anytime soon.

"Then I guess you're ahead of me." Mom took their empty cups to the sink. "Well, I think that's enough talking for tonight. I don't know about you, but I'm exhausted." Mom slipped an arm around Jennie's waist and Jennie draped her arm over Mom's shoulder. They walked through the house and up the stairs.

"Did I thank you for finding Nick?" Mom asked as they reached Jennie's door.

Jennie grinned. "Only about a dozen times."

Mom hugged her. "It's good to have you home."

"It's good to be home." Jennie had come back from her vacation ready to accept Michael into the family; now it looked like she wouldn't have to after all. Maybe Dad really would return home someday. And maybe, even though she'd signed the divorce papers, Mom would be waiting.

Jennie sat in her window seat for a while before crawling into bed. It did feel good to be home. She checked over the houses in the neighborhood. Everything looked calm and peaceful on Magnolia Street.

Three houses down, on the corner of Magnolia and Elm, the upstairs lights went on. At the same time Chuck Stuart got into his van and drove off. *A little late to be going out, but who am I to talk about being up late?* It was nearly one in the morning. Since Jennie had been on Eastern standard time for a week, her inner clock told her it was more like four.

Jennie began to lower the ivory blinds when a dark-colored car pulled into a driveway across the street. The house had recently been for sale. The real-estate sign was gone, which probably meant they had new neighbors. A figure emerged from the driver's side. From the streetlamp Jennie noticed three things. He was a male, tall, and mysterious looking. He pulled a package out of the backseat, straightened and glanced around, then crept up to the house as though he didn't want anyone to see him.

He disappeared inside and Jennie lowered the blind with a curious smile. Another mystery? Maybe.

4

Jennie awoke to what sounded like a dog's whimper. But they didn't have a dog. Through the fog of her half-asleep brain someone whispered.

"Shhh, Bernie, be quiet. You'll wake her up. Mommy said we had to be very, very quiet 'cause she's tired from her trip." One voice belonged to Nick, but the other . . . Oh, right. They did have a dog. But this was her room. What were they doing in her room?

Jennie moaned, rolled over and opened one eye. Big mistake. Two seconds flat and they were all over her. Dog licking, Nick hugging and tickling. "Help, Mom!" Jennie yelled as she yanked the covers over her head. "Nick. Stop it. I'm trying to sleep."

"Nuh-uh. You're trying to wake up. You been sleeping all day." Nick stopped wiggling, but stayed perched on her stomach.

Jennie ventured a peek at the alarm. The luminous red letters read eleven-thirty. She ducked under the covers, barely escaping Bernie's monstrous pink tongue. "Go away—and take Bernie with you. I don't like dogs licking me in the face. He smells like—like a dog."

"He needs a bath," Nick said, shifting slightly so

that his knee jabbed into her ribs.

"Ouch." She pushed his knee aside. "So give him one."

"You gotta help me. Mom says."

Great. First day home and Mom expected her to take care of Nick's dog. Whatever happened to being responsible for your own pets? Jennie heaved a resigned sigh. "Okay, I'll help, but on one condition. You get out of my room and stay out."

Nick bounced off the bed. "Come on, Bernie. She's always grouchy when she wakes up. She'll like you better after she's had breakfast."

Bernie wagged his tail and loped off, beating his master out the door.

"I am not grouchy." Jennie tossed a pillow after them. Well, maybe she was. Who wouldn't be? Jennie flung aside her cotton blanket and untangled herself from the floral print sheets. She hadn't slept well. Even with her windows open, she'd gotten too warm. Getting to bed after one in the morning and thinking about the stranger down the street hadn't helped. Jennie had considered calling the police and would have if the guy hadn't pulled a key out of his pocket and walked in like he belonged there.

A shower perked her up. She pulled on the gray T-shirt and shorts she'd picked up in the Ft. Lauderdale airport. A large circle of pink flamingoes and turquoise palm trees decorated her shirt front. Jennie took her time combing through her thick, nearly straight mane, then brought her bangs forward and braided the rest in one long braid that hung down the middle of her back.

When she'd finished, she critically examined her image in the mirror. Jennie had never considered herself beautiful, but she was quickly discovering that she did have a few assets that made her attractive to guys. Her hair for one. And her eyes. They were navy blue, like the color of unwashed denim, and fringed with dark lashes. She thought for a moment about using mascara and eye shadow, then decided against it. It wasn't like her to spend so much time in front of the mirror. Probably a result of spending most of last week in a cabin with Lisa.

Jennie glanced at the clock again. Nearly noon. She thought about calling her cousin, but decided against it. Lisa had been up late as well. She'd either be at church or sleeping. Maybe this afternoon.

She made it to the kitchen without being attacked by her brother and the beast. Mom had bacon, eggs, and toast already dished up. "This looks great. Thanks."

"I thought you might be hungry."

"How come you didn't wake me up for church?"

"Nick and I went to the early service this morning. I thought you needed your rest."

Over breakfast, she discovered that the guy she'd seen during the night was their new neighbor, Doug Reed. He and his mother had moved in four days ago. Mom hadn't met them yet, but planned to. Jennie thought it might be fun to meet them too, especially Doug. A sliver of guilt in the form of Ryan Johnson imbedded itself under her skin. It wasn't just guilt, Jennie realized. Worry had slipped in as well. Had Ryan dumped her? Was he, as Lisa had once suggested, rubbing noses with some Eskimo up in Alaska? He'd gone fishing to make money for college, but she hadn't heard from him lately, unless . . . "Mom, did Ryan call while I was gone? Did I get any mail?"

"Oh, honey, I'm sorry." Mom jumped up and hurried to the stack of papers on the counter near the telephone. "I should have given you these last night, but with Nick disappearing and all . . ."

"I got mail?" Maybe Ryan cared after all.

Mom set three envelopes in front of her daughter, then eased back into her chair. Jennie flipped through them. Nothing from Ryan. She tried not to show her disappointment as she ripped open a small envelope containing a thank-you note from Paige. Paige was a friend who'd gotten into trouble in more ways than one. "Eddie's still in the hospital," Jennie told her mom as she read the handwritten note. Eddie was Paige's boyfriend—or had been. He'd been shot in the head several weeks ago and they weren't sure he'd make it.

Mom nodded. "I've talked to his parents. He's stable, but they're concerned about brain damage. How's Paige doing?"

"She's going with her parents to Switzerland." Jennie read on. "The baby is due in December or January. She's planning on giving it up for adoption." Jennie set the card on the table and tried to put Paige and Eddie out of her mind. The choices the two of them had made had not only hurt themselves but many others as well. And it wasn't over yet.

Aside from the junk mail reminding her she could be a winner in some contest, she had gotten one other letter. Coach Haskell's scrawl reminded Jennie about swim team. This time he didn't ask her about basketball. After all the times Jennie had declined, maybe he'd finally gotten the message. Jennie took the last bite of toast, finished her milk, and pushed her chair back. She was debating whether to be mad at Ryan or to just go to her room and cry. Why hadn't he written? They'd been friends for years. Even if he had decided not to date her, he could have at least let her know. Jennie brushed off the depressing thoughts about Ryan, and after scribbling off answers to the letters she had gotten went outdoors to find Nick and Bernie.

Stepping outside was like walking into a furnace. The thermometer near the kitchen window read eighty-five. It felt more like a hundred. Jennie found Nick and Bernie waiting patiently in the porch swing. Hannah Stuart, Nick's four-year-old friend from down the street, had joined them.

"Yea! It's Jennie!" Nick and Hannah cheered as they slid off the swing. Bernie's tail whipped back and forth like a stalk of pampas grass in a forty-mile-an-hour wind. He bounced toward her and circled, slurping at her bare legs.

Hannah stood off to one side. "Can I help give Bernie a bath too?" she pleaded, fixing her huge brown eyes on Jennie.

"Sure." Jennie grinned. "But first you gotta give me a Hannah hug. I've missed you." Hannah ran into Jennie's outstretched arms and wrapped her thin ones tightly around Jennie's neck, giving her a long hard smooch on the cheek.

"Will you baby-sit me, Jennie?" she whispered.

Jennie released her. "Sure, next time your folks go out, tell them to call me."

"No," she frowned. "I mean now. I like it when you take care of me."

Jennie tousled Hannah's silky flaxen curls. "Well, I like taking care of you too, but I can't baby-sit unless your mommy and daddy tell me to." Jennie grabbed hold of her hand, then took Nick's. "Let's go wash Bernie, okay?"

Giving Bernie a bath turned out to be the most fun Jennie had had in days. He loved the water and within five minutes they were all drenched and soapy. Jennie turned on the hose to rinse the soap off the dog. "Okay, now hold still." She dropped to one knee and directed the stream of water down Bernie's back.

At that moment, the guy Jennie had seen sneaking into his house the night before roller-bladed toward them. Bernie barked. In the rush to protect his new owners, the dog decided to take the closest route. He hit Jennie with his front paws and knocked her over. Jennie landed on her rear end. Hannah squealed, Nick giggled, and Bernie bounced up to the intruder. After a perfunctory woof, he shook himself, sending a spray of water and soap suds all over the guy's legs and skates. Instead of getting mad like Jennie expected, he leaned over and rubbed Bernie's ears. "Hi, big fellow. Giving your family a bath, huh?" He chuckled at his own joke.

He was tan, tall, and well built—like he'd been working out for a long time. He was also kind of cute. Certainly not the criminal type, she decided, rescinding her impressions of the night before. His thick brown hair curled over his collar.

"Hi," he said, grinning down at her. "I'm Doug Reed—my mom and I just moved in down the street."

"McGrady." Jennie tried to get up. When her feet slipped again, she decided to stay put. "I'm Jennie." She introduced Nick and Hannah. "And that," she said pointing to the St. Bernard, "is Bernie."

Bernie woofed a greeting and took off toward the house. "Where's he going now?" Jennie asked.

"Prob'ly to eat." Nick sighed. "He's always eating. Mama says he's going to eat our house."

Jennie laughed. "You mean eat us out of house and home."

"Yeah . . . that's it. Come on." He motioned to Hannah. "Let's go watch 'im."

They disappeared into the house and Doug offered her a hand up. When he pulled, his skates slipped and he landed with a splat in the soapy wet lawn beside her. His shocked expression gave way to a smile, then laughter.

Jennie couldn't quit laughing. "I'm sorry," she managed between chortles.

"It's not that funny." He twisted around, tried to stand and fell again. On the third try he made it.

Jennie scrambled to her feet, still chuckling. "Welcome to the neighborhood. We're not usually this rowdy." Jennie found she had to look up to meet his eyes—a pale shade of blue. Jennie figured him to be over six feet. "So," she said, "where are you from?"

His eyes clouded as though he found her question disconcerting.

"Vancouver." His reply was stiff and restrained.

"Canada?"

He frowned. "No, Washington."

"Where will you be going to school?"

Doug shrugged and rubbed the back of his neck, glancing around as if he were afraid someone might be watching.

"I go to Trinity High," Jennie offered when he didn't answer. "Actually I only go part time. I'm also home-schooled since Mom needs me to baby-sit Nick. It's a good school, but it's private. 'Course, most kids around here go to . . ." Jennie let her voice trail off. Her prior suspicions were returning. *Not very talkative are you?* Jennie didn't ask the question out loud. Nor did she ask the other questions swimming around in her head, like: *Why are you acting so nervous? What are you hiding? Is someone after you? Are you breaking the law?*

"I . . . ah . . . I'd better get back." He looked back at his house. "My mom gets worried if I don't check in. I'll talk to you later, okay?"

"Sure." Jennie watched him skate off, wondering what kind of trouble he might be in and how she could find out. *Jennie McGrady,* she scolded herself, *you should be ashamed. He's probably just shy. You're making a mystery out of a molehill. Or was that mountain? Oh well. No matter.*

Doug had just moved into the neighborhood. It was far too soon to be racking up suspicions. The last thing he needed, Jennie decided, was a nosy neighbor with an overactive imagination.

She recoiled the hose and picked up the mess from Bernie's bath. Before going inside, Jennie glanced in the direction of his house again. Doug was sitting on the porch removing his skates. A woman in a blue bathrobe stood in the doorway. Jennie couldn't see her face clearly, but she did not look happy. He must have told her where he'd been because the woman glanced toward Jennie and frowned. She looked back at Doug, spun around, and went inside. Doug stood up, picked up his skates, followed her in, and slammed the door.

Just an argument between mother and son, Jennie told herself. Nothing suspicious there. So why did her intuition keep yammering warnings at her? And why, on one of the hottest days of the year, did she have a sudden chill with goose bumps to match?

5

Lisa called just as Jennie went inside to clean up.

"Allison and B.J. invited us over for a swim," Lisa explained. "Are you up to it?"

"Are you kidding? I'll meet you there in twenty minutes. Um . . ." Jennie hesitated. "I suppose I should check with Mom. She might not want to let me out of her sight."

"Tell me about it. I had to promise to be home at four."

Jennie chuckled. "And no dates for the next two weeks?"

"That's about right." Lisa heaved a long, deep sigh. "Not that I have anyone to go out with."

Lisa and Brad had broken up shortly before the cruise and Lisa still hadn't gotten over it. "Cheer up, Lisa," Jennie soothed. "You'll have tons of guys calling you this summer."

"I don't want tons of guys. I want Brad and he's at some football training camp."

Jennie shrugged. "I can honestly say I know the feeling. Ryan hasn't even written. Anyway, who needs guys? I don't know about you, but right now a swim sounds much more exciting than holding some guy's sweaty hand. I'll call you back if I can't go for some reason."

After checking with Mom and getting an affirmative response, Jennie showered, donned her blue one-piece suit and an extra large white T-shirt and shorts. She paused briefly in the living room to give Mom a thanks-for-understanding peck on the cheek and left. Driving away, Jennie waved goodbye to Nick and Hannah, who were trying to dress Bernie like a doll.

With the temperatures inching toward ninety, the Beaumont's pool seemed like the perfect place to spend the afternoon. It sure beat watching Nick and Hannah play with Bernie or sitting around daydreaming about the boy next door and a mystery that probably didn't exist.

Besides, the outing would give her an opportunity to see firsthand how B.J. was doing in her new home. Jennie and Lisa had known Allison a long time, but B.J. had only recently moved to Portland.

Talk about your blended families. Allison and B.J. had the same parents but had grown up not even knowing about each other. Their mother left home before B.J. was born. B.J. grew up poor and average looking. Allison rich and beautiful. As a result, B.J. had a chip on her shoulder the size of Texas. She and Mr. Beaumont had nearly come to blows during the first couple weeks after B.J.'s arrival.

Allison—the socially acceptable debutante—and her step-mother couldn't understand B.J.'s reluctance to become a Beaumont. For a while it looked like they weren't going to make it as a family. They still had a lot of adjustments to make, but at least now they seemed more willing to work things out.

Jennie pulled her white Mustang into the long curved driveway of the Beaumont mansion and parked behind Lisa's red Ford Taurus. The air felt oppressive. Was it just the heat?

Jennie raised her hand to knock on the door when it swung open, dispelling her somber mood. "Jennie! Welcome." Allison pulled Jennie inside and reached up to give her a whimpy hug—the kind snooty socialites bestow on each other at parties whether they liked you or not. Jennie didn't doubt Allison's sincerity, just her methods. Some things never changed.

"It's so good to see you," she chattered on. "Lisa was just telling us about your cruise. Aren't they just the most wonderful way to spend a vacation? Of course, I don't suppose being held hostage by a drug lord was all that much fun."

"It had its moments." Jennie didn't want to talk about the Caribbean for fear she'd say too much, or say the wrong thing. "How are you doing?" she asked, knowing that Allison had been through a traumatic ordeal herself only a couple of weeks before.

Frowning, Allison touched the still noticeable bruise on her cheek. "Okay. I'm not sure I'll ever get over it."

Jennie should have reassured her. Told her that bruises, especially those inside, take a long time to heal. As it turned out, she didn't have to respond.

"But I'm doing much better," Allison went on, her practiced smile back in place. "My counselor, Gloria . . . By the way, Mom and Dad appreciate you telling them about her. Anyway, Gloria says these things take time."

Jennie agreed and followed her through the house and out the open patio door to the pool area. "Make yourself at home, I'll get us some drinks. Pink lemonade okay?"

"Sure."

"Hey, McGrady," B.J. bellowed as Jennie stepped onto the deck. "Decide to lower your standards and hobnob with the rich and famous?"

Jennie grinned and tossed back a retort. "My mother always taught me to respect people on both sides of the tracks. Besides, you can't help it if you're rich." Jennie pulled off her cover-up and shorts and tossed her towel on a deck chair next to her cousin's. Lisa lay on a rainbow-colored beach towel. Her back looked warm and toasty—just waiting for a splash of cold water.

"Don't even think about it," Lisa murmured. "I still owe you for the last time."

"What?" Jennie asked innocently as she walked to the edge of the pool and cannonballed in, purposely sending a wall of water in her cousin's direction. Lisa screamed.

You are mean, McGrady, she scolded herself as she swam a couple laps. *Taking advantage of your poor cousin like that.*

It's the McGrady in you, Mom would have said. Jennie had to agree. Her mother, being a Calhoun, would never have stooped that low. By the time she reached the far end of the pool, where B.J. sat dangling her legs in the water, Jennie had forgiven herself.

"Nice shot," B.J. quipped.

"Thanks."

"But I'd watch my back if I were you."

Jennie raised herself out of the water and twisted around to a sitting position. "Did Lisa go inside for reinforcements?"

"I'll never tell." B.J. dipped water from the pool and spread it over her legs.

"You're still here." Jennie lifted her gaze to meet B.J.'s. "I half expected to come home and find you'd taken over my room." During one of B.J.'s difficult adjustment periods, she'd spent a few days with Jennie.

B.J. rolled her hazel eyes in mock exasperation. "I was tempted. But I decided to stick it out. Once they promised to stop calling me *Bethany Beaumont*, things got better."

Jennie nodded, remembering B.J.'s insistence on maintaining the name she'd been raised with, B.J. Lewis. "Your room still pink?" In their attempt to make her feel welcome, Allison and Mrs. Beaumont had decorated B.J.'s room—B.J. hated it.

"No, that's the good part. Pop—"

Jennie chuckled. "Pop? You're calling Mr. Beaumont, Pop?" Jennie tried to imagine how the middle-aged businessman with his receding hairline and three-piece suits might react.

"He hates it. Why do you think I do it?" B.J. wrinkled her nose.

Jennie had a hunch that under his pompous protestations, Mr. B. loved it. "So what about your room?"

"Oh, yeah." B.J. leaned back on her hands and kicked a fine spray of water across the pool. "When I told him I wasn't going to sleep in a pink room, he laughed and said, 'Can't fault you there.' He hates pink too. He told Mrs. B. to take me to the interior design place and pick whatever color scheme I wanted."

"What did you choose, black and orange?" Jennie teased.

B.J. punched Jennie's arm. "Just because I don't like pink doesn't mean I don't have class. Wait 'til you see it. I used neutral colors with forest accents and got this huge bear rug. And Pop bought me a six-foot-tall papier-maché giraffe."

"Sound's like a jungle. Can I see it?"

"In a minute. First I have to tell you about this guy I met. He is absolutely drop-dead gorgeous."

Allison and Lisa appeared with snacks and a tray holding four tall pink lemonades.

Allison set the tray down on a table at the far end of the pool.

Jennie and B.J. looked at each other and grinned. "Got anything against pink drinks?" Jennie asked.

"Not today. As long as it's cold and wet, I'll drink it."

They joined Lisa and Allison at the table. After taking a long swallow of lemonade, Jennie selected a peanut butter cookie from the snack tray. "You still seeing Jerry?"

Allison nodded. "Not as much as I'd like. He's really busy with the farm. About once a week we go out. B.J. and I met him and a friend of his out at Lewisville Park Friday afternoon to go swimming. We had so much fun." Allison glanced at B.J. "Did you tell them about Doug?"

Jennie raised an eyebrow in response. *Doug?* "Is that the drop-dead gorgeous guy you mentioned?"

B.J. clinked her glass on the table. "Yep. It pains me to admit it, but my dear old sis was right. She and Jerry set up this double date. At first I didn't want to go, but I figured, hey, why not? It's a hot day. If the date didn't work out, I could always hang out in the river." B.J. broke off a piece of cookie and tossed it into her mouth.

"They're perfect for each other," Allison finished, looking pleased.

"So what's his name? Do we know him?" Lisa asked.

"Doug Reed," Allison and B.J. said together.

Jennie choked on her cookie, then coughed and sputtered for several minutes trying to clear her windpipe.

Lisa slapped her on the back. "Are you okay?"

Jennie nodded. "I was before you hit me." She cleared her throat. "I don't know if it's the same guy, but Doug Reed is my new neighbor."

"You're kidding," Allison and Lisa said together.

"I just met him this morning. He's tall, nice looking, blue eyes, brown hair . . ." Jennie glanced at B.J. "About the same color as yours. He and his mother just moved from Vancouver a few days ago."

B.J. frowned. "That sounds like him. Doug said he was from Vancouver. He . . . um." B.J. shook her head. "Never mind. It isn't important."

Allison's perfect shoulder-length hair swayed as she leaned forward and placed her elbows on the table. "I think we should tell them. According to Jerry, Doug's had a rough life. His parents are divorced and he took it pretty hard. Doug got into trouble a year or so ago, but is doing okay now."

"A person's past isn't important," B.J. blurted in a defensive tone. "I don't think we should talk about it."

As much as Jennie wanted to discuss Doug Reed, she acquiesced to B.J.'s wishes, and spent the rest of the afternoon checking out B.J.'s room, swimming, and listening to Allison give Lisa advice on how to get Brad back.

———

Call it intuition or just plain curiosity, Jennie couldn't resist checking her new neighbor out. Later in the day, when she got back home, she put in a call to a friend at the police station.

"Hey, Jennie. What can I do for you?" Rocky asked. Dean Rockford had been one of the primary investigators in the Beaumont case. She and Rocky, as he'd called himself then, had gotten to be friends.

Jennie hesitated. Maybe this wasn't such a good idea.

"You're not playing detective again are you?"

"No." How she'd actually developed a crush on Dean Rockford, alias Rocky, Jennie had no idea. Actually, that wasn't quite true. Rocky was the kind of guy girls dreamed about. Older, more mature, wiser. Too old, she reminded herself. He could also be extremely bossy.

"I take it you didn't call me just to chat."

"I called to ask a favor, but never mind, you probably wouldn't do it anyway." Jennie wrapped the phone cord around her finger.

"Try me."

"Okay. We have a new neighbor. Name's Doug Reed. I just wanted to know if he had a record or anything."

"Why are you asking?"

"I told you. Just curious."

"Jennie, are you sure you're not playing detective?" Rocky's voice had taken on an even more patronizing tone. "If this guy is into something illegal, I expect you to tell me about it, not try and take him down yourself."

Jennie laughed. "You've been reading too many amateur detective novels, Rockford. I just have this feeling, you know? Like there's more going on than what he's telling his friends."

"As much as I respect your intuition, we don't have time to run checks on people because they look suspicious. Why don't you forget about this detective stuff and go find yourself a nice boy to hang around with? This Reed guy is probably acting strange because he's head-over-heels in love with you and can't think straight."

"Hardly. He's dating B.J."

Rocky chuckled. "Look, Jennie, I gotta go catch some real criminals. Take care of yourself. Bye."

Jennie gave the receiver a disgusted look and hung up. So much for having friends on the police force. Okay, so maybe she was being silly in wanting to find out more about Doug Reed. After all, solving a few mysteries did not qualify her as an expert on criminal behavior. Still, something about Doug didn't ring true, and according to B.J. and Allison, he had been in trouble. While part of her insisted she leave it alone, her detective side disagreed. *What if your intuition about Doug Reed is right?* Jennie rationalized. *What if he's using B.J. and Allison and plans to con the Beaumonts out of hundreds of thousands of dollars?* She owed it to her friends to check the guy out. And if Rocky wouldn't help, she'd have to do it herself.

6

On Monday after lunch, Lisa picked Jennie up saying she had a surprise. The surprise turned out to be a pool party at the Beaumonts'. This time Doug Reed, Jerry, and a dozen other kids had been invited. What Jennie didn't know until she walked in was that the kids were throwing a party for her.

"Jerry and I wanted to do something to celebrate being alive. And to thank you. If it hadn't been for you I'd be dead and Jerry would be in jail." Allison got choked up and misty-eyed, hugging her like a long-lost friend.

"This really isn't necessary," Jennie murmured.

Allison had no sooner released her when Jerry hung his arm across her shoulders. "I know you don't like bein' fussed over, Jen," he drawled, "but humor us. Allison's counselor thought it was a good idea. I think she called it 'closure.' " Jerry lived in the country and looked it. From his black Stetson to his silver belt buckle and western boots. He even drove a truck.

Jennie slipped an arm around his waist and hugged him back. "All right, just don't make too big a deal out of it, okay?"

The group cheered Jennie as she joined them—so much for not making a big deal. They talked about her hero status for the next half hour, then broke up to eat a dinner of hamburgers and hot dogs. Jennie decorated her plain burger with tomatoes, lettuce, onion, relish, mayo and catsup, helped herself to some potato salad and Jell-O, then looked around for a place to sit. Doug appeared at her side. "You didn't tell me you were the town hero," he said in a tone Jennie might have thought sarcastic if it hadn't been for the smile on his face.

"It's no big deal. They shouldn't be making such a fuss. Besides, what was I supposed to do? Shake your hand and say, 'Hi there, McGrady's the name, fighting crime is my game'?" She grimaced at the image.

Doug laughed. His eyes didn't. "Imagine that. A regular Nancy Drew living right across the street. I guess I'll have to watch my step."

Jennie looked him full in the eye and in a voice that half teased and half challenged said, "I guess you will."

Doug broke eye contact first and glanced over his shoulder. Jennie followed his gaze. She spotted B.J. at the far end of the pool watching them. "Look, Jennie, I know Allison and B.J. told you about me. But I've turned things around. I don't want no trouble, okay?"

The fact that he found her the least bit threatening intrigued Jennie. She didn't know how to answer. Instead of reassuring him that she didn't plan on making trouble for him, she lowered her voice and gave her best tough cop impersonation. "I'll make a deal with you, kid. Keep your nose clean and I won't have to take you in."

Going back to her true voice, she added, "In the meantime I think I'd better go straighten out B.J. Judging from the look on her face, she thinks you and I have a thing going. I wouldn't want her to get the wrong idea."

Doug muttered something Jennie didn't understand, then headed for the food table.

"What's wrong, B.J.?" Jennie asked, setting her plastic plate on the glass table top. "You look upset."

B.J. shifted her gaze from Doug to Jennie. "You don't like Doug, do you?"

"What?" B.J.'s remark caught her off guard.

"You heard me. You can be so critical and . . . judgmental."

"I don't know what you're talking about. I never said I didn't like Doug. I hardly know him. Did he tell you that?"

B.J. nodded. "At first I thought it was because he was interested in you. He kept asking all these questions. I was all ready to be jealous. But when I saw you talking to him just now, I figured it out. You two don't like each other."

"B.J., that's not true. I'm not sure I trust him, but I don't dislike him." She started to take a bite out of her hamburger.

"Jennie?" Allison interrupted, holding the phone up. "It's Rocky."

Jennie sighed, looked longingly at the burger she had yet to taste, and set it down.

B.J. gave her an appraising look. "You and he got something going?"

Jennie grinned as she scrambled to her feet. "He's a friend, B.J. Don't go getting any ideas."

"So why's he calling you here?"

"I asked him to check on something for me. To be

honest I didn't think he'd do it. Mom must have told him where to find me."

Jennie took the phone in the kitchen. "Hi. Did you change your mind?" she asked.

Instead of answering her question he asked one of his own. "How well do you know this Douglas Reed, Jennie?"

"Not very. He and his mom moved in a few of days ago. I met him yesterday. Why?"

"I don't know what tipped you off, but you were right. The kid's got a rap sheet as long as your arm. Drugs, auto theft, armed robbery, you name it. Spent the last year in a correctional facility. According to his probation officer he's been clean since his release, but guys like that don't stay clean very long."

Jennie let out a low whistle. She knew he'd been in trouble, but not that much.

"I don't know what started this little investigation of yours," Rocky added, "but I want you to stay away from him. He's bad news."

Stunned, Jennie thanked Rocky for the information and hung up. Bad news. No kidding. Now all she had to do was figure out what to do about it. Should she tell B.J. what she'd learned or wait and see if Doug really had changed?

"What's wrong?" B.J. asked. She, Allison, Lisa, and Jerry had apparently followed Jennie inside. "You said you'd asked Rocky to check something out. It was Doug, wasn't it? You asked him to check out my boyfriend."

"B.J., I . . ." It would break B.J.'s heart to know what she'd discovered, but better that than becoming involved too deeply with a criminal. Jennie repeated what Rocky had said.

B.J. did not take it well. With fists clenched, she stepped toward Jennie. "I should deck you. I can't believe you'd stoop so low. I thought you were my friend."

"B.J. don't," Allison and Lisa shouted at the same time. Jennie took a step back and collided with a chair. She fell backward, barely escaping B.J.'s right hook.

Before B.J. could attack again, Doug grabbed her from behind. Jennie hadn't seen him come in, but from the look on his face, he'd heard everything. "I don't need you to fight my battles for me, B.J. Stay out of it." Doug set B.J. aside, then glared down at Jennie. He didn't say anything. Didn't have to. The hatred in his eyes spoke volumes. He turned abruptly, stalked out the front door, and slammed it behind him. A few seconds later the tires of his car squealed down the drive.

Jennie scrambled to her feet. "B.J., I'm sorry you had to find out this way. I didn't mean for you to be hurt. But Rocky said—"

"I don't care what Rocky said!" B.J. yelled. "I'm not upset about Doug's past. I knew all about that. He told me. It's you. What gives you the right to interfere in people's lives?"

"Stop it!" Allison shouted.

Lisa hurried to Jennie's side and grasped her arm. "We'd better go."

Jennie honestly didn't know what to do or say. Allison, B.J., and Jerry were all looking at her as if she'd grown a set of horns. *I'm not the bad guy here,* she wanted to say, but didn't. Apparently they all thought differently.

"I don't get it," Jennie said, sliding into the passenger seat of Lisa's Taurus. She buckled her seat belt. "Why are they so upset with me?"

Lisa ground the key in the ignition. When the car roared to life she slipped it into gear and gunned it. "Why do you think?"

Oh, great, Lisa was mad at her too. Jennie frowned, thinking back on the situation. "Are you saying I should have played dumb and let B.J. go on dating a known felon?"

"I know you're into solving crimes, Jennie, but you went too far this time. Doug hasn't done anything wrong since we've known him. Doug and B.J. are going together. He's a friend of Jerry's. Do you honestly think Jerry would let B.J. meet someone he didn't trust?"

Jennie braced herself as Lisa slammed on her brakes at a red light. "We don't know that he hasn't committed a crime since he's been out. I saw him sneaking into his house the first night we were home. Maybe Jerry doesn't know everything Doug was into."

"*Was*. That's the operative word here, Jen. As in the past. Doug is trying to start over. Sneaking into his own house doesn't make him a criminal. You and I have done that. He and his mom moved so he could have a fresh start in a new neighborhood and school. You pretty much ruined it for him."

"We all knew he'd been in trouble. Since his past wasn't a secret, how could I ruin it? Seems to me he messed up his own life by getting into trouble in the first place."

Lisa opened her mouth, then closed it again while she maneuvered the car into a left-hand-turn lane. She waited until she'd executed the turn before speaking again. "Jerry told Allison and me that the cops patrolling Doug's neighborhood—one especially—had been giving him a really bad time. Harassed him constantly. Doug and his mom moved so he could get away from the guy. He still has a record, of course, but the police here don't know him—at least they didn't until now."

Jennie leaned her head against the seat. "The police don't hassle people without a reason." Even as she jumped to the officer's defense Jennie's own inner voice condemned her. *You brought in the police, McGrady. They'll be watching every move he makes, just waiting for him to make a mistake.*

Lisa dropped Jennie off at home and left without even saying goodbye. It hurt having Lisa angry with her. But her hunches about Doug had been right on. He was not the kind of guy B.J. should be associating with.

On the other hand, maybe B.J. had been right in calling her critical and judgmental. She did have high standards. Did she expect too much of people? Okay, maybe she had gone too far in calling Rocky. If Doug had changed, and really was trying to start over, Jennie owed him an apology. The only way to know for sure would be to talk to him.

Doug's car, a dark green, older model Cutlass, was parked in his driveway. Jennie made an abrupt turn in front of her porch, crossed the street, and hurried up the sidewalk to Doug's house. Everything was out in the open now. They could be honest with each other. If he really wanted to make amends, Jennie would do whatever she could to help him.

She rang the doorbell three times before anyone answered. The woman she'd seen the day before appeared in the same blue bathrobe, the same tangle of brown, uncombed hair. Too late, Jennie remembered what Mom had said about Doug's mother being a nurse and working nights. "Oh, Mrs. Reed, I forgot. I'm sorry if I woke you. I was looking for Doug."

Mrs. Reed shook her head as though she had no idea what Jennie was talking about. She ran a hand through her hair and stifled a yawn. " 'Scuse me," she mumbled. "I work nights this month." Then rubbing her eyes, she added, "Doug must not be home." Then in an annoyed tone muttered, "If you find him, tell him he'd better get home and do his chores."

Mrs. Reed closed the door before Jennie could respond. Jennie glanced up and down the street, thinking Doug might be roller-blading. When she didn't see him, she headed back home. Strange. His car was there. Could he be avoiding her?

Jennie couldn't blame him if he didn't want to talk to her. Vowing to try again later, she crossed the street and paused to talk to Nick and Hannah, who were riding bikes on the sidewalk in front of the Stuarts' house—not an easy task with a St. Bernard puppy bouncing around in front of them.

She was just climbing up the steps to the porch when an overwhelming sense of uneasiness ripped into her with the intensity of a lightning bolt. She'd felt it before. Each time it precipitated something terrible.

Jennie glanced back at Doug's house. The blinds in the second-story window moved. At least she thought they had. Would Doug be angry enough to hurt her? Maybe he was up there right now, watching her, taking aim, getting ready to shoot.

Jennie hurried inside and closed the door, shutting out the deadly thought.

7

"Nick? Is that you?" Mom called from the kitchen.

"It's me." Jennie slipped off her sandals, willed her heart to slow down to a normal pace, and shuffled down the hall toward her mother's voice. "Nick is playing with Hannah," Jennie added. "Do you want me to call him in for dinner?"

"In a few minutes. Why don't you fix a salad and set the table first?"

Without answering, Jennie opened the refrigerator and took her time pulling out the ingredients for salad. The cool air felt good on her hot skin.

"Did you have a nice time at the Beaumonts'?" Mom asked. "I thought you'd be having dinner there."

Jennie grimaced, part of her anxious to relate her news about Doug, part of her afraid to.

"Okay, what happened?"

Mom would have made a good detective. She always seemed to be able to read minds. "I got thrown out before I could eat," Jennie admitted.

"Should I be shocked?"

"I blew it, Mom. They all hate me." Jennie went on to tell her mother what had happened and what she'd learned about their new neighbor.

While her mother didn't have any brilliant solutions, Jennie felt better having talked about it. Mom didn't seem too thrilled about having a delinquent living in the neighborhood, but thought as Lisa did, that he deserved a chance to start over. Maybe Jennie had been too hasty in calling Rocky, maybe not. Time would tell. In the meantime, she'd try to settle things with Doug and the others. After dinner.

At six o'clock, Jennie stepped onto the front porch and called Nick in to eat. When he didn't answer, she jogged down the steps and across the lawn to the sidewalk where the children had been playing earlier. Nick and Hannah were no longer riding bikes. Jennie slowed her pace, having worked up a sweat in the hot, humid air. Only Jennie didn't feel sweaty. A chill sliced through her. She again glanced toward Doug's house, surprised and at the same time relieved to see that the car was gone. She took a deep breath and let it out slowly. *McGrady, you're letting your imagination get the best of you. Just stop it.* Jennie shook away the sense of foreboding and continued up the Stuarts' walk, then detoured to the backyard.

"Nick!" she called. When he still didn't respond she knocked on the back door. No one answered. She peeked into the garage window. Both cars were gone. Nick must have gone home the back way while she'd come around front.

Jennie hurried back to the house. "Mom? Did Nick come in?" she asked as she stepped into the kitchen.

"No." Mom frowned. "He's not outside?"

"I didn't see him. The Stuarts aren't home."

"Well, check his room. He might have come in while we were talking."

Jennie hurried up the stairs, calling his name as she went. Nick wasn't in his room, his secret place, under his bed, or in the bathroom. "C'mon, Nick. Quit fooling around. It's dinner time."

"Nick?" Mom called, joining Jennie in the search.

A half hour later, they'd gone from being annoyed to being concerned to being worried. After they'd checked the house, yard, and neighboring yards for the third time, Jennie followed her mother into the house. "Do you think we ought to call the police?"

Mom shook her head. "I don't know. I hate to call them and end up finding Nick in another one of his hiding places. I was so embarrassed the other day."

"But what if he's really missing this time?"

"You're right. I can't think about how it might look. I'm getting worried."

Jennie opened the cupboard, took down a glass and filled it with water. "Nick was playing with Hannah just before I came in. Could he have gone somewhere with them?" She tipped the glass up and chugged down half a dozen gulps.

"I suppose it's possible, but he knows better. Anne would never take him without calling me. I'm sure he's around somewhere."

Frustration and worry had tied the knots in Jennie's stomach into a giant macrame wall-hanging. "Maybe we should call Michael in case Nick got it into his head to go visit him."

"No. Nick hasn't mentioned Michael all day." She paced back and forth across the kitchen floor. "Still, it's been almost an hour." She glanced up at Jennie, unspoken fear evident in her eyes. "I hate to admit it, Jennie, but I don't know what else to do. If Nick really is missing, we could be wasting valuable time. I think we'd better call the police."

"And Michael," Jennie added, setting her glass in the sink. "He'll want to know."

Mom sighed. "I suppose you're right."

Michael pulled into the driveway ten minutes later and apologized for taking so long. Jennie was filling him in on the details when a police car pulled up in front of the house.

"Hi, Jennie," the officer greeted when she opened the front door.

She hardly recognized Rocky in his uniform. His long sun-bleached ponytail had been replaced by a buzz cut. Jennie felt some of the knots in her stomach loosen. She wasn't sure whether to hug him or shake his hand. She did neither. Instead, Jennie smiled and nodded. "You going to help us find Nick?"

"Hope so. Usually when we get a call about a missing kid, they're in the house or in the neighborhood somewhere. Your mother says you found him Saturday night."

"I was lucky."

"Let's hope your luck holds out."

"It's starting out okay. You took the call."

"Actually, that wasn't luck. I wanted to see where this Reed guy lived. I was only about a block away when your call about Nick came in."

"Yeah." Jennie shifted her gaze from Rocky's face to her shoes. "I need to talk to you about him. First though, we'd better find Nick. He's been gone over an hour."

Rocky quickly greeted Mom and Michael, then he

and Jennie went back over the house and grounds. When they didn't find Nick, Rocky placed a call to his supervisor, then took out his pad and pen. "Looks like you'd better give me some more of the details. You first realized he was missing around six?"

"I called him in to wash up for dinner," Jennie said. "When he didn't answer, I went over to the Stuarts' to get him. They weren't home. At first Mom and I thought he'd pulled the same stunt as he had the other day. But he isn't in any of the places he likes to hide out. He wasn't with any of the neighbors either. The last time I saw him was in front of the Stuarts' house. I'd just gone over to talk to . . ." Jennie didn't finish.

Rocky lifted his gaze from his note pad to her eyes. "What's wrong?"

"I . . . nothing." Jennie stammered. "I'd gone over to talk to a neighbor. Nick and Hannah were riding bikes." Jennie didn't mention the confrontation she'd had with Doug earlier in the day, or her fleeting thought that Doug may have taken Nick to scare her or to get even. She didn't mention it because she was already in trouble with her friends for having Doug checked out. If she told Rocky what she was thinking, and Doug turned out to be innocent, they'd never forgive her. She also wanted to give Doug the benefit of the doubt.

"Could the Stuarts have taken Nick with them?" Rocky asked.

Mom shook her head. "Not without telling Jennie or me. He wasn't supposed to go anywhere else," Mom said. "He knows better." She stared at her hands then looked up, glancing at Michael, then Rocky. "You must think I'm a terrible mother. I try to keep track of him, but . . ."

Rocky stood. "Try not to worry, Mrs. McGrady. I'd like you to stay here in case he comes back or calls. Jennie, Michael, maybe you can comb the neighborhood again. Alert all the neighbors. He's got the dog with him—and his bike—that's a good sign. Since he went into hiding the other day, my guess is he's done the same thing again, but we don't want to take any chances."

Lisa, Kurt, Aunt Kate, and Uncle Kevin came in as Rocky left. Mom had called them after talking to the police. Uncle Kevin gave Jennie a hug, then turned to Mom. "You holding up okay, sis?"

Mom nodded. "I don't know whether to be angry or scared. Nick's never acted like this before."

"Let's not worry prematurely," Kate said, wrapping her arms around Mom. "He's five—they can start getting pretty independent at that age. He may have decided to go to the store or something."

"Where's Gram?" Jennie asked. Gram was usually the commanding force in a family crisis and Jennie missed her calming spirit—not to mention her knowledge of police matters and what, at times, seemed to be a direct connection with God.

"She and J.B. are on their way to the coast. Gram was anxious to get home." Kate rubbed the back of her neck and tipped her head from side to side. "I left a message on her answering machine. Let's hope we find Nick before they get there. I hate worrying her, and knowing Gram, she'll want to come back tonight."

Uncle Kevin, an airline pilot, took over the job of organizing everyone, telling them they needed to go through the same process as before. After praying, Lisa and Jennie combed the neighborhood again. Kevin and

Michael took Kurt with them to drive around to the area and check the stores.

To Jennie's surprise, Allison and B.J. showed up to help look for Nick. Lisa had called them. They acted as though the argument they'd had earlier in the day had never happened. Jennie was more than willing to let it go.

Allison went with Lisa to cover the blocks north and west while Jennie and B.J. took the southern and eastern side. Within a half hour, they had twenty people canvasing the neighborhood. Nearly everyone they questioned, though they had no new information on Nick or Bernie, joined in the search.

Jennie and B.J. were heading back to the house when Doug pulled into his driveway. He climbed out and jogged toward them. "What's going on?" He looked from Jennie to B.J. "I thought you two were mad at each other."

"McGrady can be a pain," B.J. said, "but her heart's in the right place. Anyway, her little brother is missing. A bunch of us are looking for him."

Doug frowned. "The little guy with the dog?"

Jennie studied him intently, trying to read his reaction. She wanted to ask him where he'd been. His leaving at the same time Nick disappeared was too much of a coincidence to ignore. "His name is Nick. The last time I saw him, he was playing on his bike in front of the house on the corner. Did you see anything unusual—anyone who shouldn't have been there?"

"Why don't you just ask him, McGrady?" B.J. ran a hand through her permed hair. Her hazel eyes flashed with annoyance. "You think Doug had something to do with your brother's disappearance, so just ask him.

I'm sure Doug doesn't have anything to hide."

So much for the subtle approach. Jennie took a deep breath and plunged in. "Okay, I admit I'm suspicious. I came over earlier to apologize for what happened. Your car was here, but you didn't answer the door. Later, when I went to look for Nick, your car was gone. I thought you might be mad enough to get back at me."

"You're right about the first part," Doug said, avoiding her eyes. "I didn't answer the door. I didn't want to talk to you. I was pretty upset, but I wouldn't hurt a little kid. I saw them playing in the front yard, too. After you went back to your house, I saw this skinny blond lady standing in the doorway talking to them. They were gone when I left about fifteen minutes later."

"Probably Mrs. Stuart. What time did you leave?" Jennie asked.

"Around six."

"Where were you going?"

"I had a job interview." He grinned at B.J. "I got it. I'll be working at Hammond's Construction." Doug folded his arms and looked Jennie in the eye. "Look, I didn't do nothin', okay? You can call Hammond's. They'll tell you I was there."

"We believe you. Don't we, Jennie?" B.J. settled a case-closed look on her that intimated an end to the conversation. Jennie let it go. She'd call the company later and confirm Doug's story.

"I . . . um . . ." Doug shifted uncomfortably beside B.J. "Look, Jennie, I don't know if it means anything, but on my way to the job interview, I . . . I might have seen Nick's dog. A St. Bernard pup was running down the street about a block from here. Looked like he might have been heading for the Crystal Lake Park."

8

Jennie grabbed his arm. "Was Nick with him?"

"I just saw the dog. He was probably chasing a car or something."

"Are you sure?"

"Look, I'm sorry about your brother," Doug said. "But that's all I know. And just to show you I don't hold any grudges, maybe I could, you know, help look for him."

His concern seemed genuine, and though she didn't completely trust him, Jennie welcomed his company in the search. "Thanks. I'd like to check out the park next. Nick loves it there. Mom won't let him go there alone, but he might have figured that if Bernie went with him it would be okay. And if the dog you saw was Bernie, Nick would have been following him. I'll need to let Mom know. Can I use your phone?"

Doug let her in and pointed toward the back part of the house. "It's on the kitchen counter," he explained, then went back outside to talk to B.J. The living room looked like it hadn't seen the business end of a vacuum cleaner in a month. Newspapers littered the floor. Dirty dishes cluttered the countertop and sink.

No wonder Doug's mom had asked her to send him home to do his chores. *Don't be so critical, McGrady. So they're messy. That's no reason to be judgmental. If it weren't for Mom, you might be messy too.*

Jennie retrieved the phone from under a soiled dishtowel and punched out the number. "Any sign of him?" she asked when Kate answered.

"Not yet, sweetie."

After letting Kate know where she was going, Jennie hung up. Before joining Doug and B.J. on the front porch, she offered up another plea. "Please, God, please let us find him. Keep Nick safe."

Jennie swallowed back the growing anxiety. They should have found him by now. Why hadn't they? She'd hung tightly to the idea that Nick had just wandered off and that she'd find him playing with Bernie in the park. Jennie tipped her head back and took a deep breath, willing herself not to cry, then joined Doug and B.J.

"They haven't found him yet, have they?" B.J. asked.

"No. I'm going to the park now. You don't have to come."

"I know. I want to." B.J. turned back to Doug. "You coming?"

"Sure. Count me in." Doug started down the walk, then turned back. "I'd better tell my mom."

Jennie watched him go inside.

"You still don't trust him, do you?" B.J. asked, hands on her hips as though she were expecting a fight.

Jennie shrugged. "Not completely."

"You're wrong about Doug. He's a neat guy and deserves a chance."

"Everyone deserves a chance, but be careful, B.J. We don't know him all that well."

Before B.J. could answer, Doug appeared in the doorway. "I can't go. I'll explain later." He closed the door.

B.J. and Jennie looked at each other. "Weird," B.J. said. "I wonder what that was all about."

Jennie shrugged. "Maybe his mother needed him for something." *Like cleaning the house.* "Let's go. I want to search the park before it gets dark."

The eighty-acre park was only a few blocks from Jennie's house, and by the time she and B.J. arrived, Lisa, Allison, Uncle Kevin, Michael, Kurt, and six other people had come to help them search. They spread out, looking in and around the trees and bushes, the bathrooms and other outbuildings. By 8:45, the search party had dwindled to police, family, and a few friends. After searching for two more hours and finding nothing, Michael suggested they go back to the house. Jennie watched his Adam's apple rise and fall, and followed his gaze to the large pond that covered much of the park's acreage. "You don't think he's in there . . ."

"Let's hope not." Michael led her away from the water. "I'm still hoping he's off chasing Bernie somewhere, or that your neighbor has taken him shopping. I'm going to round up the others. We need to regroup and decide what to do next."

When he'd gone, Jennie sat on a bench near the park entrance, trying to put her chaotic thoughts in order. With so many people around and so many scenarios about Nick's disappearance, that wasn't an easy task. Had Nick gone somewhere with Anne and Hannah Stuart? Jennie doubted it, but let herself believe it anyway. She glanced at her watch. If Anne had taken Nick and Hannah shopping, she'd be home by now. Jennie imagined herself and the others trudging home, only to find Nick asleep in his bed.

Before Jennie could take her imaginings any further, Lisa, Allison, and B.J. appeared on one of the paths leading out of the park. "We gotta go, Jen." B.J. hunkered down beside her.

"But we'll come back in the morning," Allison assured. "That is if you need us. Hopefully he'll be home by then."

"You ready to go," Lisa asked when they'd gone, "or do you plan on camping out here all night?"

Visions of Nick being home spurred her on. "Let's run."

Lisa groaned an objection, but followed her anyway.

Jennie slowed as she approached the Stuart house. It still stood dark and empty.

"Jennie, are you coming?" Lisa asked.

"Be there in a minute." Where had the Stuarts gone? Was Nick with them? *You know what happened, don't you?* she directed her silent questions at the house. Its windows gazed out at her like eyes, taunting her, refusing to reveal its secrets. *Oh great, McGrady, now you're talking to houses. You are one big certified nut case.* Jennie turned from it and hurried into the warm glow emanating from the windows of her own house.

Aunt Kate brought a tray of sandwiches into the living room where they'd all gathered to watch the news.

"Thanks, hon," Kevin said, taking a bite of his

sandwich. "We'll get some rest and go out again tomorrow."

"Come on," Kate coaxed when neither Lisa or Jennie moved toward the food. "You girls need to eat."

Their voices seemed far away. Kate was right. They did need to eat—to keep up their strength. Maybe that would clear her mind. But she wouldn't be able to sleep. She'd sneak out and keep looking. Maybe they'd overlooked something.

But what? Not even the blood hounds from the search and rescue team had picked up a scent. The flyers had gone out and local news stations would begin broadcasting the story. Jennie forced herself to eat the roast beef sandwich, washing it down with a glass of milk someone handed her.

At eleven they watched as the newsanchor introduced the story. "On a tragic note tonight," the somber-faced newscaster said in a voice that sounded as if she really cared, "Police and dozens of volunteers are searching for five-year-old Nicholas McGrady, who disappeared around six this evening. Authorities fear the child may have wandered away from his home in the Crystal Lake area late this afternoon." A recent picture of Nick flashed on the scene. Nick's bright eyes and mischievous smile belied the seriousness of the situation. "Nick was last seen wearing a black Mickey Mouse T-shirt. His bike and a St. Bernard puppy named Bernie are also missing. Anyone with information on the boy or the dog is urged to contact the police immediately."

Jennie tuned out the rest of the news. None of it mattered. Nothing mattered except finding Nick. Though police had already covered the roads he might have taken to the church and Michael's house, Jennie intended to try them again. Even if Nick hadn't talked about Michael today, he could have decided to go see him.

Jennie made it as far as the front door before Mom, Aunt Kate, and Lisa stopped her. "I can't let you go out again," Mom said. "I know what you're feeling. I don't want to stop looking either, but—"

Jennie stared at her mother. "How can you say that? We can't give up."

"We're not giving up. We have to be sensible." Mom's eyes looked tired and red rimmed from crying. Jennie should have hugged her instead of arguing.

"Your mother is right," Aunt Kate interrupted. "We're all bushed. We'll be more help to Nick if we pace ourselves."

"But we can't let him stay out all night. He'll be scared and cold."

"He has Bernie to keep him warm. And it's summer." Kate reached out and drew Jennie into her arms. "I don't like it any more than you do."

"Come on, Jen," Lisa insisted, "we'll rest awhile, then I'll go back out with you." Too exhausted to fight them and knowing deep down they were right, she followed Lisa upstairs and went to bed.

———

Sometime later, Jennie awoke with a start, her heart hammering as though she'd just run a marathon. Nick. She had to find Nick. Jennie rolled over to her side and looked at the luminous red numbers on her alarm clock. 3:00. She'd been asleep for over three hours. *You have to get back out there, McGrady.* Her mind raced, but her body felt like lead.

Jennie sat up and swung her legs off the bed. Carefully stepping over Lisa, she made her way to the window seat. The three-quarter moon lit up most of the yard, casting long shadows across the lawn. Nick was out there somewhere. She sat on the cushions and leaned her head against the window, willing her mind to connect with his. "Where are you Nick? What's happened? Tell me how to find you? Did you leave us a clue?"

Jennie caught a movement out of the corner of her eye. A shadow stretched over the grass as someone dressed in dark clothes emerged from the side of the house, crossed the street, then disappeared behind a hedge. Jennie hurried back to her nightstand, picked up the phone and dialed 9–1–1.

9

"What's going on?" Lisa moaned.

"Somebody's snooping around outside. I called the police. You can go back to sleep."

"No way." Lisa scrambled out of her sleeping bag. After pulling on sweats, they tore down the stairs and waited for the police to show up.

"Could you tell who it was?" Lisa asked as they watched a squad car creep toward them. A spotlight illuminated houses and yards as the officer cruised by.

"I didn't get a good look at him." An image of Doug flashed through her mind. Jennie dismissed it. Doug may not be the greatest guy in the world, but that didn't make him responsible for every criminal activity in town.

The officer turned off the searchlight and pulled up to the curb in front of Jennie's house. Jennie and Lisa met him halfway up the walk.

"Hello, again." Robert Beck, the officer who'd investigated Nick's first disappearance, glanced at his note pad. "You reported seeing a prowler?"

Jennie explained what she'd seen.

"He's probably long gone by now. You two go back

inside. I've called for backup. We'll have another look around and let you know if anything turns up."

When another officer arrived they went out on foot.

"Want some hot chocolate?" Lisa asked.

"Sure. Might as well. I can't go back to sleep."

"I'm surprised our moms are still asleep. My mom wakes up if I turn over."

"Yeah. Mine too. I'm kind of glad." Jennie took a pan from the lower cupboard near the stove while Lisa got the milk. "They looked really tired."

They'd just heated the milk when Michael and Uncle Kevin walked in the back door. Judging from their rumpled appearance and the circles under their eyes, they'd neglected their own advice and had been out all night. Jennie offered them the hot chocolates she and Lisa were fixing.

"Thanks." Uncle Kevin patted her shoulder. "What I need is coffee—hot and strong."

"I'll make it," Jennie offered. She didn't ask them if they'd found anything. Didn't have to.

The men sat at the table with Lisa, while Jennie measured out the coffee, poured water into the reservoir, and turned it on. Instead of sitting at the table, she hoisted herself onto the counter. When Michael asked about the police cars out front, Jennie told him about the prowler. She'd just finished when someone knocked on the back door.

"Just came back to tell you we have a suspect," Beck informed Jennie and the others when he came in. "Found him sitting on the back steps of one of the houses across the street. Took off running when he saw us." Beck shook his head. "When we caught him he tried to tell us he lived there and had locked himself out."

"Who is he?" Jennie asked.

"A punk kid—new in the neighborhood. Got a record as long as your arm. Name's Doug Reed."

Guilt tore at Jennie's reserve. Had she been too quick to call the police? Doug had become a friend of sorts, and Jennie didn't want to make things worse for him. Still, if he'd been snooping around . . . "I met him the other day. He does live there. His mom works nights."

"You say he has a record?" Uncle Kevin sounded upset.

"Word is he was recently released from a correctional facility up north," Beck offered.

"What did he do time for?" Michael asked.

"Auto theft." Beck stepped back toward the still-open door. "Well, I'd better be going. You folks take care."

Michael stopped him. "Officer, do you think he had anything to do with our missing boy?"

"I wouldn't speculate on that. But you can be sure he'll be questioned about it."

When Officer Beck had gone, Kevin sank back in his chair. "Does your mother know about this Reed kid?"

Jennie nodded. "We talked about it yesterday."

"The police should have questioned him immediately," Michael said. Uncle Kevin agreed. It seemed strange having her previous suspicion of Doug voiced by someone else. She'd pretty much ruled him out as a suspect. Now the possibility crept back in and with it a feeling she couldn't grasp. Part of her wanted to jump to Doug's defense. He'd seemed concerned and had even offered to help. *Yes,* Jennie reminded herself, *then he backed out. Face it, McGrady, you don't know Doug all that well.*

"Jennie?" Michael asked. "What is it?"

She shifted her gaze from his shirt collar to his eyes. He looked worried—of course he did. They all did. "I . . . you don't really think Doug . . . I mean—he has a record, but he's not a . . ." The dark thoughts were too terrible to say out loud.

"Doug didn't have anything to do with Nick's disappearance," Lisa insisted, giving Michael and her father a hostile look. "If the court thought he was dangerous, they wouldn't have released him. Nick just wandered off. I know we'll find him, just like we did before. Maybe he's asleep somewhere and pretty soon he'll wake up and come home. He'll wonder what all the fuss was about."

Her reasoning wasn't quite right. Criminals did get out of prison. Jennie could have argued the point but didn't. Lisa knew the truth as well as she did.

Uncle Kevin took a deep breath, looked at Michael, then into his coffee cup. "Of course Nick is okay. We'll find him." He took a sip and set the cup back down.

Lies, a voice in her head thundered. Maybe they were all kidding themselves, but thinking anything else was simply not an option. People just didn't go around hurting cute little kids like Nick.

Kevin and Michael left the kitchen, saying they needed a couple hours of sleep. After they'd gone, Jennie sipped at her lukewarm cocoa. Frustration dug into her like a wood tick. She plunked her cup down and shoved it to the center of the table. "We're wasting time just sitting here." Jennie barely recognized the hard-edged voice that escaped her throat. "We should be out there looking. I'm going to walk around the block. Maybe we missed something."

Lisa rubbed her eyes and yawned. "It's still dark."

"Fine. You can stay here. Go back to sleep if you want," Jennie snapped. "I'm going out." Hostility oozed through her like molten lava. Jennie grasped the back of her chair, staring at her white knuckles. *What is going on with you, McGrady? You blew up at Mom last night. Now you're doing the same thing to Lisa.* She took a deep unsteady breath. "Lisa, I'm sorry. I didn't mean to snap at you. I just feel so . . . I don't know . . . helpless, I guess. And scared. I have to keep going. Part of me wants to cry—another part wants to bash everyone's head in. It's hard to explain."

"Hey, it's okay. You're worried. You have a right to be upset." She glanced down at her cup. "I'm scared too, Jennie. I couldn't bear it if anything happened to Nick."

Jennie released the back of the chair. "I'd better go."

"Do you think it's safe? Maybe we should wait until morning."

"It is morning. It'll be light soon." Jennie pushed her chair back and stood. "Are you coming?"

"Sure. I guess. I'm not going to let you go out there alone." Lisa rinsed their cups and left them in the sink. While Lisa went to the bathroom, Jennie slipped upstairs to retrieve their tennis shoes and socks and waited for Lisa on the front porch. The morning air smelled crisp and fresh.

The sun had begun its ascent, tossing hues of yellow and orange into the predawn sky. Lisa emerged from the house and sat down in one of the white rattan chairs to put her socks and shoes on. Jennie straddled the railing beside her, staring at the spot where she'd last seen Nick. "I wonder where they are."

"Who?" Lisa asked as she finished tying her shoes. They left the porch and started down the walk.

"The Stuarts. Mom and I thought Nick was there, but when I went to get him, they weren't home. They still aren't home."

"You think they might have Nick with them?"

"We keep coming back to that. It's a possibility, I suppose, but Mrs. Stuart would never just take Nick—not without talking to Mom." Jennie stopped in front of the Stuarts' house.

"Could Nick have told them your mom had given him permission?" Lisa asked.

"I don't know. To go for ice cream or to the store maybe, but they've been gone too long for that. It's been twelve hours."

"Nick could have stowed away," Lisa suggested. "He could have hidden in the backseat or something."

"They would have seen him by now and called. Anyway, that doesn't make sense."

"None of this makes sense." Lisa kicked a pebble from the sidewalk into the street.

Jennie grabbed Lisa's arm. "Wait. I just thought of something. Maybe Nick is in the house. He could have been playing in a closet or something and got stuck or locked in. Mr. and Mrs. Stuart may have taken off, not knowing he was there."

"It's possible, isn't it? Are you going to call the police and have them check the house?"

Jennie chewed on her lower lip. "I don't know. I think they'd have to get a search warrant and that could take hours. Nick could be hurt or something. Maybe I could just go in and look around."

"You mean break in?"

"No. Mom has a key. They usually ask her to water plants and pick up mail when they're gone. They didn't do that this time. I wonder why?"

The windows of the Stuart home faced east, reflecting the rising sun. Was it a sign? With renewed hopes as high as her heart rate, Jennie told Lisa to meet her in the backyard, then returned to her own house.

The Stuarts' key was hanging on a peg just inside the back door on the wall above the telephone. Good old organized Mom. She always insisted on hanging the keys there. Being involved with a neighborhood watch program, Mom had keys to three of the neighbors' houses. The Stuarts, the Whites, and the Murrays. And all of them had a key to the McGrady house.

Jennie grabbed the key with the tag that read "Stuart—back door" and raced across the lawns to where she'd left Lisa.

"Are you sure you want to do this?" Lisa asked. "I mean, like . . . what if we get into trouble?"

Jennie twisted the key into the lock, turned it, and pushed the door open. "We won't. Trust me." Warm, stale air greeted them. Having been there numerous times to baby-sit Hannah, Jennie knew the house nearly as well as her own. It was newer and smaller than Jennie's, not as many nooks and crannies to hide in.

"Let's start with the garage," Jennie said. Making an abrupt left at the kitchen sink, she opened the door to the double-car garage. Dark rust-colored stains marred the otherwise clean concrete floor. Someone had recently sprinkled on the stuff her mom used to absorb oil leaks. Shelves and hooks lining the wall kept everything neatly stored. Jennie closed her eyes trying to remember what she'd seen there before. She opened them and stared at a blank space along the back wall. "Bikes," she said, walking toward the area where they normally hung. "They always keep their bikes on these hooks when they aren't using them."

"Maybe they're on vacation."

Jennie shook her head. "They'd have told Mom. And besides, both cars are gone." Going back into the house, Jennie left Lisa to search the main floor while she went upstairs to check the bedrooms. The doors were all closed except for the master bedroom. A twinge of guilt trickled through Jennie as she opened the closet doors. Jennie ignored it. The his and her walk-in closets held nothing but the usual clothes, shoes, and accessories—*a place for everything and everything in its place*, as Mom would say. Anne Stuart separated her clothes by type. Evening dresses on one end, followed by church clothes, and so on, ending with casual shirts and slacks. Several gaps toward the casual end, along with the missing bikes, seemed to confirm the vacation theory. But why hadn't they told anyone?

Chuck Stuart's closet left Jennie with the same impression, though it was more difficult to tell since he had less closet space and fewer clothes. She was about to move down the hall to Hannah's room when she spotted Lisa coming up the stairs. "Find anything?"

Lisa shook her head. "No, but they sure are neat. Can you believe it? Even the laundry is all caught up."

"You should see their closets," Jennie said as she walked into Hannah's room. "Whoa. Talk about contrasts." The small room reminded Jennie of a doll house. Puffy Priscilla curtains adorned the windows and a pair of pink ballet slippers hung above the bed next to a large framed pastel of a ballerina. That's where the doll-house look ended.

Toys and clothes were strewn all over the floor. Three of the drawers in Hannah's white dresser had been pulled out.

"This is really strange." Jennie peered into the closet. "Most of her clothes are gone." She dropped to her knees. "I don't see her dolls. Hannah keeps a big suitcase full of dolls in here."

Jennie heard footsteps on the stairs. Panic exploded in her chest like gunfire. She pulled Lisa into the closet and yanked the door closed.

10

Jennie held her breath as the door she'd just closed swung open.

"Find anything interesting?"

Jennie's gaze traveled from the shiny black shoes, up the pressed blue uniform, past the grim mouth, and into Rocky's piercing blue eyes. She gulped and offered a wane smile. "We . . . I . . ."

"Spit it out, McGrady. What are you two doing here?"

He was still holding on to the door and Jennie ducked under his arm. He gestured for Lisa to come out as well. She did. "We weren't doing anything wrong," Lisa said staring up at him with the same wide-eyed expression Jennie had seen her give traffic cops who had the nerve to stop her. "Since Nick was here last, Jennie thought he might have gotten locked in . . . or something." Her voice trailed off when Rocky glared at her.

He turned back to Jennie. "I should haul you in for breaking and entering."

But he wouldn't. Jennie's heart settled back into its appropriate cavity. "I didn't break in. I have a key. How did you know we were here?"

"Funny thing. I was driving by and saw lights in the window. I figured either the Stuarts were home or they had a prowler."

"Guess we shouldn't have turned on the lights."

"You *should* have talked to your mother—or to me—first. It might have saved you some time."

"What do you mean?"

"What I mean," he drawled, "is that we searched the house last night."

"Oh." Jennie frowned and added, "I thought you needed a search warrant or something. That's why I decided to do it myself." Embarrassed at being caught, Jennie looked down at their shoes—her worn, dingy white Nikes, his polished black ones.

"We don't need a warrant in a case like this. When a child is missing, we can go in if we have reason to believe he might be there."

Jennie knew what Rocky would say next. The last thing she needed was a lecture on leaving the investigation to the police. When Rocky didn't chastise her she lifted her gaze to his face. His features had softened and his eyes were no longer a stormy gray, but warm as a summer sky. Jennie nearly melted. *Oh no, Mc-Grady, not again. You are not going to humiliate yourself again by drooling over a guy who's too old for you.* Still, when he looked at her like that—like he cared . . . Jennie broke eye contact. *Forget it, McGrady.* Jennie mentally whacked herself alongside the head as if to dispel the ridiculous path her thoughts had taken.

"Isn't this where you're supposed to tell me to stop playing detective?" she asked sarcastically.

"Ordinarily I would, but we're talking about a

missing child here. With all the dead ends we're coming up against we need all the help we can get."

Rocky then surprised her by pulling a pad and pen out of his shirt pocket. "So, Sherlock, what did you and Watson here find that Portland's finest might have missed?"

He was baiting her. Challenging her to hold on and not be discouraged. Jennie shifted her thoughts from not finding Nick in the house to the possibility that she might be able to piece some clues together. "Most of Hannah's clothes are gone. So are some of Mrs. Stuart's. It looks like they went on a trip."

Rocky nodded. "We suspected that. We're checking it out now. So far all we know is that Chuck Stuart took a few days off work. Apparently they didn't bother to let anyone know where they were going. Anything else?"

"Their bikes are missing. All of them—not just Hannah's and Nick's."

He raised an eyebrow. "Mr. and Mrs. Stuart both had them?"

Jennie nodded. "They biked a lot. Nick sometimes went along when they went to the parks around here." As Jennie pictured the garage another realization came to mind. "The cars. Both cars are gone." Jennie recalled seeing Chuck Stuart leave the night she got home. "If they went on a trip they wouldn't need both cars."

"Unless they had to leave at different times," Rocky made a note on his pad.

"Hannah's room. It's really messy—everything else is neat. I don't know if that means anything. Her doll case is missing, too. It's like they planned to be gone awhile. I know it doesn't make much sense, but do you think it's possible they took Nick with them?"

Rocky shrugged. "We'll know soon enough. We're calling their friends and relatives now. We should be able to locate them fairly soon."

Rocky escorted them out of the house and back to Jennie's, then left. Jennie sat on the porch next to Lisa and watched until the taillights disappeared around the corner of the next block.

"What is going on between you two?" Lisa asked.

"What? Who?" Jennie leaned forward and wrapped her arms around her knees.

"You and Rocky. And don't try to deny it. I saw the way you looked at each other."

"I've been trying to figure it out myself."

"You're mom would never let you date him, you know."

"I don't want to date him, Lisa." Jennie stared at a spot where the paint had started to peel and picked at it. "I think it's because he's a cop, you know. Maybe we're like—kindred spirits." Her thoughts about Rocky slid out of focus. She felt guilty again. *What's with you, McGrady. You shouldn't be out here thinking of how you feel about Rocky. You need to concentrate on finding Nick.*

Lisa rested her head on her knees. Her eyes drifted closed. She stifled a yawn and mumbled, " 'S'all right. You don't have to tell me. I'm sorry, Jen. I can't stay awake anymore."

"Then go to bed." Jennie ruffled Lisa's already mussed-up curls. "It's okay, really. Thanks for hanging in there with me."

Lisa muttered something that sounded vaguely like

"you're welcome," then stumbled inside.

Jennie stood and stretched. She needed something to revive her. Food maybe. Or a shower. Hushed voices and the smell of bacon coming from the kitchen told Jennie her mother and Aunt Kate were up. For some reason, the thought of facing Mom tied her stomach in knots. Instead of heading into the kitchen, she went upstairs to Nick's room. Jennie scooped up Nick's blanket and Coco and climbed into Nick's bed. She'd only intended to stay a minute, but her eyes drifted closed and opening them again required more strength than she could muster.

Two thoughts pierced Jennie's mind as the need for sleep dragged her into the darkness. In one, Nick was crying. "I need my blanky. I need Coco." Jennie reached out to put her arms around him and hugged his blanket closer.

Suddenly Nick was gone and Jennie heard her father's voice. "I have enemies, Jennie. I can't come home. I can't take the chance."

———

Jennie awoke to car doors slamming and a flurry of voices. Gram. Everything would be okay now. Jennie couldn't remember what was wrong, but something had to be. She snuggled deeper under the covers. Coco's furry head was lodged against her arm. The satin binding of Nick's blanket lay under her cheek. Nick's bed. What was she doing in Nick's bed? And where was Nick? She sat up and rubbed her eyes. Her head ached and her mouth felt like something had died in it. Jennie crawled out of bed and stumbled into the bathroom.

Her brain kicked in as she showered. So did her

memory. Wrapped in a large blue towel, Jennie exited the bathroom and went into her room to change. Lisa was still asleep. According to the clock on her bedside stand—which read 10:00—and the sun trying to sneak between her blinds, they'd been asleep for nearly three hours. She threw on a pair of shorts and what she hoped would be a matching shirt, grabbed a brush, and tried to get her tangled hair into a pony tail.

Not even Gram's presence could raise Jennie's hopes. She felt frozen inside. It was the same kind of sensation she'd had after being told that Dad's plane had gone down in Puget Sound. The one thing that had kept her going was faith that he was still alive. He had been. He still was. Dad hadn't come back, but at least she knew the truth. Things would work out with Nick too.

The thought she'd had just before falling asleep that morning came back to haunt her. Nick's disappearance could have something to do with her father. *You're way off base, McGrady,* she told herself. *Dad wouldn't let something like that happen.* Jennie yanked the snarls out of her long hair, wishing she could discard her thoughts as easily. Unfortunately, it could happen. It had happened to her. One of Dad's enemies had gotten to her on a Caribbean cruise. He'd been arrested, but according to her father there were others. Jennie wished she could contact Dad, but that wasn't possible. By now he had a new identity and only an elite few knew it. Besides, trying to contact Dad could place him and their entire family in danger again.

Pony tail in place, Jennie walked over to the pictures she kept on top of her dresser. She picked up the one of her father. His dark blue eyes smiled back at her.

He didn't look the same now. His beautiful black hair, or what was left of it, had been tinted brown to help conceal his real identity. But she talked to the photo anyway. "What do I do now, Dad? What if someone took Nick to get back at you?"

She was surprised at how quickly the answer came. *You have to talk to Gram. There's no other way.* "Sorry, Dad," Jennie murmured as she set the picture back. "I know I said I wouldn't, but I don't know what else to do."

Jennie went in search of her grandmother. Somehow she'd have to get Gram away from the others so they could talk. "How about a run?" she suggested when she found Gram in the kitchen.

"I'd like that." Gram set her coffee down and turned to Mom. "You don't mind, do you, Susan?"

"Of course not." To Jennie she said, "You should eat something first." Jennie drank a glass of milk and ate a piece of peanut butter toast, then headed for the door.

During their run, Jennie told Gram what had really happened in the Caribbean. "I'm afraid one of Dad's enemies might have kidnapped Nick."

"I can see . . . why you'd be concerned," Gram puffed.

"You don't seem surprised—about Dad, I mean . . . you already knew all that, didn't you?"

Gram nodded. "Not officially. As far as the federal agencies are concerned, I don't." Gram slowed to a walk. "I'm not sure Jason knows I recognized him. Although I doubt he'd be surprised. I am his mother, you know."

"I wondered." Jennie eased back to stay in step with

her grandmother. "What are we going to do, Gram? What if it is one of Dad's enemies?"

"J.B. and I have already discussed the possibility, but I'll talk to him again. I do know that he's alerted his contacts in both the FBI and the DEA."

"So what do we do in the meantime?"

"We try to find Nick."

"Gram . . ."

She gave Jennie cautioning look. "The less said, the better. I promise I'll let you know if I hear anything."

It wasn't the answer Jennie wanted, but it would have to do. They didn't talk much during the rest of the three-mile run. As they neared Magnolia Street, a powder-blue van pulled into one of the driveways. Jennie stopped.

"What is it, dear?" Gram asked. What's wrong?"

"The Stuarts." Jennie broke into a run. "They're back."

11

By the time Jennie reached them, Chuck and Anne Stuart had gotten out of the van and were pulling out their bags.

"Mr. and Mrs. Stuart," Jennie gasped, still out of breath from her run. "I'm so glad you're home. We've been frantic. We were afraid something might have happened to you."

"Whoa," Chuck said, lifting a hand to stop her. He grinned at Jennie, a set of perfect white teeth showing off his tan. "Slow down, girl. Anne and I just went to the beach for a couple days."

Jennie went still. A chill swept through her bones. Chuck had said *Anne and I*. Jennie glanced at the bicycle rack on the front of the car. It held only two bikes—and neither of them belonged to the children. And they only had one car.

"Hannah's not with you?"

"No," Anne responded. "Since you were gone when we made plans, I asked my sister to stay with Hannah. As often as Hannah and Nick play together, I'm surprised you didn't know."

Gram came up behind Jennie, cupping her hands

on Jennie's shoulders. She greeted the Stuarts and asked, "Then you haven't heard?"

Anne shook her head, setting her shoulder-length straight blond hair into motion. "Heard what? What's going on?" She had perfect hair, like Allison's. Only Allison had the flawless face of a model. Anne looked like she'd been on too many unnecessary diets.

"Nick's missing. The police have been looking for you. It's been in the papers and on the news."

"Missing?" Anne's pale green eyes widened in alarm, taking up nearly a quarter of her face. "I thought you found him."

"We did, the first time. But on Monday he disappeared again."

"That's terrible, but why would the police be looking for us?"

"We thought perhaps you'd taken Nick with you," Gram answered.

"The last time I saw him was on Monday," Jennie said. "He and Hannah were playing in front of your house. When I went to call Nick in for dinner he was gone."

"Are you telling us Cathy and Hannah aren't here either?" Chuck asked.

"I didn't know you had a sitter," Jennie explained. "I thought you were here and that you'd taken Hannah somewhere. No one's been here since Monday night."

Anne glanced up at her husband, then at the house. "We'd better call my parents. Cathy and Hannah may have gone there."

"Could she have taken Nick, too?"

"Oh, Jennie. I doubt that."

"Well, I don't," Chuck grumbled. "That airhead is liable to do anything."

"I know you're anxious to get in touch with your sister," Gram said, "but I wonder if you could tell me when you left on your trip."

"Saturday night." Chuck's voice had taken on a hard edge. "Actually it was Sunday morning." He gave his wife a frosty look. "We didn't get out of here until one in the morning."

"I saw you leave." That had been the night she'd come home. "But you were alone."

"I . . . I wasn't feeling well," Anne offered apologetically. "I was lying down in the backseat."

"We don't want to intrude," Gram said, giving Jennie's shoulders a squeeze, "but do you mind if we come in while you make your phone calls? We'd like to know whether or not Cathy took both children."

"Sure," Chuck grumbled, making it clear that he did mind, but manners prohibited him from saying no.

Anne made the first call to her parents. Worry drew deep lines in her forehead. She hung up the phone. "They haven't heard from Cathy in over two weeks. They said to tell you both hello. They heard about Nick on the news and wanted you to know they're praying for your family."

"I'm sorry, I don't understand." Gram frowned. "Do I know your parents?"

"Oh, you may not have made the connection. My maiden name is Williams. My folks run a Bed and Breakfast in Bayview."

"Bob and Emily. Of course."

Jennie knew Anne's parents, but didn't really know all that much about their private lives. Jennie remembered meeting Cathy Williams several years ago. Ryan had known her from school. Tall, blond, and slender, Cathy resembled Anne. So Doug's description had been accurate. Jennie had just pictured the wrong woman.

"You haven't?" Anne's question brought Jennie back to the present. "Are you sure?" After mumbling a thank you into the phone, Anne hung up. When she looked at her husband, the concern in her eyes had advanced to fear. "Her roommate at the college hasn't seen Cathy since Saturday afternoon when I picked her up." Chuck balled his hands into fists, his dark eyes narrowed in anger. "I knew we couldn't trust her. We should have waited until Jennie could sit for us. So help me, Anne, if that screwball sister of yours has done anything to my kid, I'll . . ." It seemed to take all the power Chuck Stuart had to reign in his anger. Jennie had never seen him this way. He'd always seemed pleasant. But then Jennie knew firsthand how easily fear and worry could turn to anger.

Gram stepped toward Chuck and placed a hand on his arm. "Mr. Stuart," she said, in a calm and steady tone. "I can understand how upset you must be. Cathy may have taken the children, but the possibility remains that she and the children may be in danger. I suggest you put aside your differences and call the police."

Gram's no-nonsense approach seemed to settle him. "You're right." He lowered himself into the nearest chair and rubbed his forehead. "I'm sorry. The thought of losing my little girl . . ."

"D—do you want to call?" Anne stammered as she picked up the phone. Her hands were shaking so hard, she nearly dropped it again. "Or do you want me—"

Chuck grabbed the phone from her. "I'll do it." At the same time he stood and placed an arm around her shoulders. "You'd better sit down. You look like you're ready to collapse."

Anne lifted her shoulders like a turtle retreating into its shell. She left Chuck's side and sank into the couch. The cushions nearly swallowed her slender frame.

Fifteen minutes later, a female officer Jennie hadn't seen before responded to the Stuarts' call. After questioning them, she went out to her cruiser and radioed in a report.

Dozens of new questions surfaced. The most pressing one lodged in Jennie's mind centered around Anne's sister. Had Cathy Williams taken the children? Why? From the conversation, Jennie had pieced together a picture of Cathy. Cathy Williams, 19, sophomore at Pacific University in Forest Grove. Good grades, no priors, not even a suspicious boyfriend, that Anne knew of anyway.

"We should be going." Gram nudged Jennie. "I'm sure you'll be wanting to get unpacked."

Jennie wasn't ready to leave, but obediently followed Gram to the door.

"I'm curious." Gram stepped onto the porch and turned back to Anne and Chuck. "It seems rather odd that you'd leave for your trip so late at night."

"Chuck's been working evenings at the store. Since he had to catch up with some paperwork before he could leave, he didn't get home Saturday until almost midnight."

"It's no mystery." Chuck appeared behind Anne. "I

like to get as much time at the place I'm staying as possible. I also like to rest several hours before I have to go back to work. And I do need to work this afternoon." He started to close the door. "So, if you'll excuse me. I'd like to get some rest."

"Of course." Gram turned to go, then back again. "Oh, just one more thing. What beach did you say you'd gone to?"

A look of irritation crossed Chuck's handsome features. "I didn't say. And frankly, I resent your questions."

"Chuck, please," Anne interrupted. "We have nothing to hide. We were staying at a private cottage near Manzanita." The door closed, abruptly ending the conversation.

As they were leaving, Jennie tossed Gram an admiring look. "You reminded me of Columbo back there." She slouched her shoulders, squinted one eye, and lowered her voice. " 'Oh, one more thing.' " In her normal tone she asked, "Why were you asking them so many questions."

Gram smiled. "Not a bad impersonation. I'm not really sure why I questioned them. Habit, I guess. And intuition. Something isn't right between those two. I'm sure you noticed it too."

Jennie nodded. "They were both acting strange. But what about Cathy? Do you think she could have taken the kids?"

"It's hard to say. According to Anne, no. But Chuck seems to think otherwise. We'll just have to see what the police turn up."

"The Stuarts are back," Jennie informed her mother as she and Gram entered the kitchen. The matter-of-fact tone in her voice surprised her. "Hannah and Anne's sister, Cathy, might be missing too."

"I know. Officer Beck came to talk with me while you were over there." Mom sounded detached, like she'd closed herself away. Jennie couldn't blame her.

"Where is everyone?" Jennie asked.

"Kevin and Michael are out with search teams— I'm not sure where. Kate's gone to the store." Mom brushed her hair from her forehead with the back of her hand. "Oh, Helen, that reminds me. J.B. had to leave. He wants you to call him at the office."

"I hope they're not sending him on another assignment. Not now." She sighed, finger-brushing her newly cut salt and pepper hair. "I suppose I'd better call. Do you mind if I use your phone, Jennie? I'd like to leave the main line free."

"Sure." With J.B. working for the FBI, his urgent call could have been about anything. She just hoped it wasn't bad news about Nick.

Not sure what she should do next, Jennie watched her mother cut up a chunk of meat for stew. "Are you going out again?" Mom asked.

"They're searching in so many places, I don't know where to go."

"Lisa called earlier. She's at Crystal Lake with Allison and B.J. . . ." Jennie didn't wait for her mother to finish. The message had given her direction.

Two hundred people had volunteered to help in the widening search. The police had gotten dozens of phone calls in response to the radio and television newscasts and flyers. Searchers covered several parks in the area, but most of them—Jennie and her friends included—shifted their focus to a three hundred and fifty acre section of woods five miles away. Someone had reported seeing a boy fitting Nick's description near there. The boy had been riding a bike. The blood hounds hadn't picked up Nick's scent, but the description had been so close, the police decided to search the area anyway.

At the twenty-four-hour point, authorities declared Cathy and the children officially missing. By nightfall, most of the volunteers had gone home to their families. A few, those groups prepared to work in shifts, would continue to search through the night. None of the leads had panned out, and they were no closer to finding Nick than they had been when they discovered him missing.

Jennie had gone back to the Crystal Lake area around 8:30 and had spent the last hour at the park watching divers scour the lake. Lisa hadn't left her side all day. Neither had B.J. and Allison until a few minutes before when they'd apologized for leaving and gotten into the black sedan Mr. Beaumont had sent. They'd offered Jennie and Lisa a ride, but Jennie declined.

Michael had been there too, holding his breath along with the others whenever a diver brought up an article of clothing, an old boot, a toy. "Come on, girls," he said. "We'd better get back to the house. I promised your mothers I'd have you in by ten—it's almost that now."

The scene was like a rerun of the night before. They were even using the same words. "You girls want a ride?"

"No thanks," Jennie said. "I need to walk."

Lisa groaned. "We've been walking all day."

"You go ahead. I'll meet you back at the house."

Before Michael could object to Jennie's being alone, Lisa conceded. "No. I'll come with you."

When Michael had gone, Jennie dragged in a deep breath of cool crisp air. The temperature had dropped from the high eighties to the mid-sixties. Not cold, but enough to make her shiver. "Want to run?"

"Sure, why not. I'm too exhausted to walk."

As they ran, Jennie let her mind drift back over the events since Nick's disappearance. Why weren't they finding anything? "Maybe we're not trying hard enough," she murmured, wishing she could think more clearly.

"Did you say something?"

"No . . . yes." Jennie paused at Magnolia and Elm to check for traffic. "This searching isn't getting us anywhere. Maybe we're not trying hard enough." Jennie sprinted the last few yards across her lawn and stumbled on the front porch steps. Instead of getting up, she turned around and sat on them.

"Not trying . . ." Lisa gasped, dropping down beside her. "How can you say that?"

"I know, everybody's been working hard, but it's not enough. There has to be something . . ." Jennie stopped to listen. "What was that?"

"What? I didn't hear anything." Lisa stiffened.

"It sounded like someone crying."

"Jennie, in case you haven't noticed, everyone around here has been crying."

"No, not like that." Jennie heard it again, a faint whimpering sound. "It's coming from over there." She sprang from the porch and began searching through the shrubs lining the porch. Lisa followed suit, starting at the corner and working back toward Jennie.

"Jennie . . . I think you'd better come here." The catch in Lisa's voice hit Jennie with knife-sharp accuracy. Jennie didn't even want to think about what her cousin may have found. When Jennie reached her, Lisa was down on her hands and knees in front of the large rhododendron that stood at the corner of the house. "Under there."

Jennie dropped to her hands and knees and crawled under the dense shrub to the cavernous open area inside. Her hand touched something furry. "Is it him?" Lisa asked, spreading the branches to afford Jennie some light.

Jennie closed her eyes hoping what she'd seen wasn't real. She opened them again. Her stomach recoiled, threatening to empty its contents. Bernie lay curled in a heap, his once brown and white fur matted with dried blood.

12

"Get help. Quick. Tell them—" But Lisa had already gone. Just as well. At that moment Jennie couldn't give voice to her thoughts.

She clenched her teeth, willing her stomach not to ache, her heart not to break, and her eyes not to cry. *No, don't think about it. Nick's okay.* "Nick's okay, isn't he, Bernie? You're going to be all right."

Needing to concentrate on anything but Nick at that moment, she leaned over and placed her ear against Bernie's rib cage. His heartbeat was faint, but steady. At least he was alive. Nick would be too. Afraid to move him, Jennie sat beside the pup, stroking his fur.

"She's under there." Lisa had come back.

The bushes parted and light from two flashlights streamed in. Jennie shielded her eyes against it. Michael crawled in beside her. As if he knew what she'd been thinking, he placed an arm around her shoulders. "This might not have anything to do with Nick. Maybe Bernie got hit by a car and crawled here."

Jennie nodded. "Dogs will do that, won't they?" She let herself believe Michael's words, even though deep inside, she feared they weren't true.

"Stay strong, Jen." Michael gave her shoulder a squeeze. "We'll find him. In the meantime, we'd better get Bernie to a vet."

Jennie pinched her lips together. Stay strong. Yes. She could do that. *You have to, McGrady. You have to for Nick—and for Mom.* Michael lifted Bernie into his arms and carried him into the open. Jennie followed.

"Here, I'll take him." Uncle Kevin lifted the dog out of Michael's arms. "Any idea what happened?"

"Looks like he's been hit on the head." Michael repeated his theory about a car.

"Too bad you can't talk, little fella." Kevin stroked Bernie's head. "We'd better wake the others to let them know. Maybe you and the girls can do that while I get Bernie to the vet."

Uncle Kevin called their veterinarian and left a few minutes later.

Jennie looked up at Michael, sensing that he expected her to go back to the house with him. The last thing Jennie wanted to do was be with her mother when they broke the news about Bernie. Mom would fall apart. Gram might too. And that would be her undoing. "If you don't mind, I'd rather to stay out here while you tell them."

A look of understanding passed between them. Michael started to go, then turned back. "Don't shut her out, Jennie. She needs you. You need each other."

"I know." When Michael had disappeared inside, Jennie sank onto the step. "This is crazy, Lisa. I'm almost afraid to think about what happened."

"Maybe we're better off not thinking too much. Maybe we just need to keep looking."

They sat on the porch swing together, trying not to

think. They'd agree to wait up for news about Bernie. In less than an hour Uncle Kevin returned.

"What did Dr. Phillips say?" Lisa asked.

"Is Bernie going to be okay?" Jennie held her breath waiting for his answer.

"She thinks he'll survive. Looks like Michael's theory was right," Kevin told her as he wrapped his arms around both girls and drew them inside. He waited until they were in the living room with the others before going on.

"Bernie's injuries seem to indicate that he was hit by a car. He's got a concussion and a number of bruises. Only Doc Phillips doesn't think he could have crawled very far. A few feet maybe."

Doug had seen Bernie over a block away. "So how did he get under the rhododendron?" Jennie asked. "We checked those bushes yesterday. He wasn't there."

Mom was not taking the news well. "I don't know how much more of this I can stand." She broke into tears again and Michael pulled her into his arms. The tragedy seemed to be drawing them together again.

"Doc thinks he might have been hit yesterday." Kevin focused his gaze on Michael's face. "I'm only guessing, mind you, but it looks like someone picked him up after they hit him and brought him here."

Then what happened to Nick? The question seemed to hang in everyone's mind, but no one asked it. Jennie felt the urge to escape this company of mourners. Didn't they know—couldn't they feel it? Nick was still alive. Even if they'd found Bernie it didn't mean Nick had been hurt too. They were so ready to believe the worst—especially Mom.

Jennie would have preferred being alone for a few

minutes, but Lisa followed her out and sat on the steps next to her. "Mom sent me out to see if you were okay." As she spoke, her gaze drifted from Jennie to the vintage green Corvette pulling up in front of the house. "Who's that?"

"Rocky."

"What's he doing here?"

"I don't know. Maybe your dad called the police to tell them about Bernie."

Rocky climbed out of his car and came toward them, wearing jeans and an Oregon State T-shirt. In his hand he held a small plastic bag that swayed from side to side as he walked.

Jennie's heart stopped. She forgot to breathe. He hadn't said a word, but she knew. He was there to tell them something about Nick. Something Jennie didn't want to hear.

"Is your mother home?" he asked, his face somber, his features like granite.

Jennie nodded. "I thought you were off duty."

"I am. I asked to be notified if there were any breaks in the case."

"What happened?" Jennie asked, swallowing back waves of nausea. "Did you find Nick? Where is he?"

"Jennie, stop. I need to talk to your mom." Jennie led him into the house. Mom and the others were still gathered in the living room. Jennie leaned against the wall and waited. Lisa glanced at her. She felt it too. They all did, Jennie realized as she looked at their faces.

"Mrs. McGrady," Rocky began. He glanced around at the others, then placed the bag he'd been holding on the coffee table. "We got a tip about two hours ago from a woman who said she'd seen a boy fitting Nick's description in Washington Park, near the zoo." Rocky took a deep breath and let it out again. "She reported seeing a man with him."

"A couple of guys went to look around and found this. The lab guys found traces of blood on it. We think it might be Nick's."

Jennie's hopes flatlined the second Rocky lifted out the black shirt. On the front was a neon Mickey Mouse.

"Dear God, no." Michael covered his face with his hands, but not before Jennie saw the anguish written there. Mom stared at the shirt like she'd been cast in stone, then crumbled. Jennie bit her lip to stop herself from screaming—to somehow keep the pain inside from being real. The shirt was the one Nick loved most. Michael had given it to him for his birthday. It was the last thing she'd seen him wearing.

"Is he . . . dead?" Michael asked.

Jennie clamped a hand over her mouth to hold back the storm building inside her. Michael had pulled the dreaded words out of Jennie's mental closet and marched them out in front of everyone where they stood naked and ugly.

Memories of three other missing boys ripped into Jennie's brain. The bodies of two small boys had been found in a park just across the river in Vancouver, Washington. Another boy had been abducted, and . . .
"No!" Jennie hadn't meant to say it out loud. When she realized she had, she added, "You can't mean that. Nick is alive. He has to be."

13

After Rocky had gone, Jennie went upstairs to wash her face. "What are you going to do?" Lisa hugged a teddy bear she'd grabbed from Jennie's collection. "I mean . . . you'll be okay, won't you?"

Jennie shrugged. "I'm not going to kill myself if that's what you mean." At Lisa's stricken look, Jennie tipped her head back and groaned. "I'm sorry. I shouldn't have said that."

"Please, Jennie, just promise me you'll be okay."

"Don't worry. So they found a shirt. It may not even be Nick's."

"Mom and Dad want me to go home. I need some clean clothes, and to be honest I think we're both getting a little ripe. I'll be back in the morning. I can stay here though if you need me."

Jennie gazed into her cousin's green eyes trying to focus. Lisa looked pale and exhausted. "Maybe you should rest tomorrow. You look beat."

"Jennie. This is Nick we're talking about. I'm not giving up as long as there's a chance we'll find him."

"Thanks."

"Yeah, now go take a shower and get some sleep.

You're beginning to smell like yesterday's road kill."

They went back outside, and when Lisa and her family had gone, Jennie closed her eyes and leaned her head against the porch railing. *You gotta get back out there, McGrady. You've got to keep looking.* She envisioned herself going to the park where the police had found Nick's shirt. Then common sense kicked in. *No. Lisa's right. Shower first. And get some rest.* She'd feel a whole lot better and be able to think more clearly after a shower and some sleep.

The shower refreshed her. Instead of going to bed, Jennie decided to look around outside again. She walked over the ground where she and Nick had given Bernie a bath, then wandered to the place she'd last seen Nick and Hannah playing. Their laughter echoed in her mind and sliced through her heart. "Help me out here, Nick. I know you're out there somewhere. What happened to you?"

Jennie was just heading back to her house when a taxi pulled into the driveway. Someone got out, paid the driver, and collected a large duffle bag from the backseat. Judging from the lean, tall shape she guessed it was a man. He had his back turned, so she couldn't be certain. He turned toward Jennie as the cab drove away. The streetlight made his golden hair shine like a halo. Jennie couldn't have been more thrilled if the visitor had been an angel. In fact she'd have been disappointed. He saw her about the same time she recognized him. He dropped his bag on the sidewalk and ran toward her, stopping only a few inches from where she stood.

"It's about time you got here, Johnson." She raised her hand to brush aside a tear.

"I left as soon as I heard." Ryan closed the distance between them and pulled her into his arms. Jennie circled his waist, resting her head against his broad shoulder. After a moment he backed away and dropped his arms to his side. "I probably smell like fish."

"Maybe a little, but I'm not complaining."

He reached out and tucked a strand of hair behind her ear. Jennie swallowed. The butterflies were back. He bent and kissed her. Soft, gentle, warm. He was everything Jennie remembered and more. When he lifted his head he smiled. "I've been waiting a long time to do that, Jennie McGrady."

Jennie only half smiled. "I'm glad you're here." Not even Ryan could completely ease the pain she'd been experiencing since Nick's disappearance.

As if reading her mind, Ryan swung in beside her and hung an arm around her shoulder. "I'm sorry about Nick."

"How did you find out?" Jennie asked as she slid her arm back around his waist.

"I talked to my mom. Grabbed the first flight I could get. The cab driver told me the police haven't been able to find him. I was hoping maybe you had better news."

Jennie shook her head, not trusting herself to speak. "I'll tell you about it later." When they reached the drive, Ryan released her to pick up his bag. He slung it over his shoulder and followed Jennie inside. After getting the traditional McGrady greetings of hugs from Gram and Mom and a handshake from Michael and J.B., Jennie showed him to Nick's room. He freshened up while Jennie changed Nick's bed.

"I'll bet you're exhausted," she said when he came

in. "If you want to go to bed now . . ."

"No. I couldn't sleep. I'd rather sit with you for a while—that is if you're up to it."

"I was hoping you would," she said, leading the way back downstairs. "We have a lot to talk about." She left Ryan in the entry, went to the kitchen to get a couple cold drinks, and told her family she and Ryan would be on the porch.

Sitting on the porch swing with Ryan, Jennie almost felt happy, which made her feel guilty. It seemed strange to feel so good and so bad all at the same time.

"I can't believe you're here. I was beginning to think you didn't like me anymore."

Ryan frowned. "How could you think that?"

"You never answered my letter for starters."

"Oh, that." He winced. "I guess I'm not much of a letter writer. Besides, it was hard to put what I wanted to say into words. I guess I'm more a man of action." He settled an arm around her and she leaned against him. They sat together in silence, letting the wooden swing carry them back and forth.

They belonged together, Jennie decided. Like old friends—okay, more than friends. It felt so good having him there. Jennie's fear of losing him melted away like snow in the sun.

"I know it's hard for you to talk about it, and you don't have to, but I'd really like to know what happened to Nick. In fact, I want to know everything that's happened since we last saw each other."

"It would take a month to tell you everything."

"How about we start with Nick. That's the most important."

Jennie took a deep breath and plunged in. During

the telling, they heard Michael leave. The lights in the spare bedroom went on for a while, then off, indicating Gram and J.B. had gone to bed. Mom came out to remind her not to stay up too long.

Shortly after one, Jennie finished her story. "So there you have it," she concluded. "You know as much as I do, which isn't a lot. We don't have much to go on."

In the last few minutes, Ryan had taken to wrapping strands of her hair around his fingers. After a while he dropped her hair and reached down for her hand. He wove his fingers between hers and held it up between them. "Jennie," he said, locking his gaze on hers. "I know solving one mystery together doesn't make us experts. And to be honest, I didn't do all that much of the solving. But we made a pretty good team when Gram disappeared. We can do it again."

Whether it was the strength in his hand or the sincerity in his eyes, Jennie felt almost invincible. Maybe they could make a difference. Maybe they could succeed where everyone else had failed.

After deciding they'd be much better investigators in the morning, they turned out the lights and went upstairs. "Feel free to use the bathroom up here. I'll use the one in Mom's room or the one downstairs." She reached for the light switch in the bathroom and flipped it up, grabbed her toothbrush from the holder on the counter, and opened her bedroom door. "Night," Jennie whispered. She waited until he found the light switch in Nick's room, then stood for a moment outside her mother's room. She'd avoided Mom most of the day. Now she felt guilty and something else. She wanted to share the strength she'd found in being with Ryan.

Opening the door, Jennie crept in. "Mom," she whispered—loud enough to be heard if Mom was still awake, but quiet enough not to wake her if she'd fallen asleep.

"Come in, sweetheart," Mom whispered back. The stained-glass bedside lamp washed the room with dozens of warm colors. "Want to crawl in here with me?"

Jennie's immediate reaction was to say no. It had been a long time since she'd been in her parents' bed. When she was little she used to snuggle in between them after a bad dream. She wasn't little anymore, and she wasn't having a bad dream. Reality was much scarier. "Sure," she agreed. "Just let me get my pajamas and brush my teeth."

Jennie returned to her room and got ready for bed. She felt embarrassed about going back into Mom's room, but managed to convince herself that with Nick gone, Mom needed her.

———

Daylight brought warmth, but little else. Whatever strength she'd found in Ryan's presence the night before had disappeared with the darkness. She awoke at seven A.M. in her mother's queen-sized bed. Mom was already gone. Jennie wished she could stay holed up under the fluffy down comforter all day. But Ryan was there. He'd come to help. The thought motivated her enough to get up and dressed.

Gram and Mom were the only ones in the kitchen when Jennie arrived. "How would you like to take a drive in the country?" Gram asked. "I've been talking to Susan about it and she thinks it will do you a world of good."

"A drive? How can you think of going for a drive—" Seeing the scheming look in Gram's eyes, Jennie grinned. "Never mind. I think a drive is just what we need."

"Good. We'll see if Ryan and J.B. would like to accompany us."

Their drive just *happened* to take them west on the Sunset Highway to the Pacific University campus where Gram and J.B. located the names and phone numbers of Cathy's professors. Ryan and Jennie managed to locate and talk to Cathy's roommate, Angela Jones or Angie, as she preferred to be called. Actually, she talked to Ryan—couldn't take her eyes off him. Jennie wondered what Angie would think if she knew Ryan was about two years her junior. Unfortunately, Jennie was never able to work it into the conversation.

The girls shared a house with two other female students, both of whom had gone home for the summer. She and Cathy were taking summer classes. Angie explained all that in one breath as she led Ryan and Jennie into the small living room that looked like a reject from the psychedelic sixties. "Would you like something to drink?" she asked.

"Diet Coke if you have it." Jennie folded her long self into a florescent pink beanbag chair, hoping she wouldn't look too ridiculous getting up. Ryan said he'd settle for anything as long as it was cold and non-alcoholic. Angie seemed to think that was hilarious. Ryan sank into the lime green bag next to Jennie. When Angie left the room he leaned toward her. "Can you believe this place?"

Before Jennie could respond, Angie came back with their drinks—three cans on a tole-painted wooden tray, which she placed on the floor in front of them. She took a can of root beer, popped the top, and dropped to the floor, crossing her shapely legs as she went down. She ended up about six inches from Ryan's lap. "I hope you'll forgive the mess. I'm getting ready for a show. I'm majoring in art."

And minoring in men, Jennie thought as she opened her can of Coke and took a drink. Warm. She glanced at Ryan. His can was so cold it was already sweating. "What can you tell us about Cathy?" Jennie asked in a voice she hoped was more friendly than her thoughts.

Angie gifted Ryan with an impish grin. Jennie could have sworn she batted her eyes. "Cathy's like really nice. Smart too. I mean she's majoring in psychology." She laughed. "We make a good team. I'm mostly right-brained. You know—creative. She's mostly left—analytical."

That didn't fit Chuck's description of *airhead* and *screwball*. "So, you'd consider her pretty stable?"

"Stable?" Angie shrugged. "I guess that depends on what you mean. She's like dependable, you know. You can trust her."

"But . . ." Ryan supplied the transition and Angie went with it.

"She picks these loser guys. The last one slapped her around a couple of times. Her shrink thinks it's because her dad was such a strict disciplinarian."

"Does she have a boyfriend now?" Jennie tried to shift into a more comfortable position, only managing to sink deeper into the chair.

"Who doesn't? I mean right now I don't, but then I'm not looking."

I'll bet. Jennie pinched her lips together to keep from making the comment aloud. "But Cathy did. What was his name?"

"Judson Miller. He's a senior. A law major, I think. In fact, I was really surprised she took that baby-sitting job. They were supposed to get together on Monday." Angie shrugged her shoulders and leaned closer to Ryan. "She must have forgotten. Judson came by to pick her up. She hadn't said anything to me. Naturally, I didn't want him to think she stood him up, so I told him where she was."

"Did he seem upset?" Jennie asked.

"That's putting it mildly. After he left I got worried—you know, like maybe I shouldn't have told him where to find her. I got to thinking maybe she didn't want him to find her."

"When did he leave here?"

"You don't think he . . ." Angie left the question hanging there like a threatening black cloud.

Jennie's thoughts raced ahead. Could Judson have gone to the Stuarts' in an angry rage? Could he have forced Cathy to go with him at gunpoint? If so, what had he done with the children?

14

For the first time since they'd come in the room, Angie looked at Jennie. "He left around two . . . yes that was it." She turned back to Ryan. "I was baking a pie and the buzzer went off." She scrambled to her feet. "Would you like a piece?"

"We really don't have time." Jennie tried to jump up too, but her bare legs stuck to the vinyl beanbag chair, dumping her in an ungraceful heap at Ryan's feet. She shouldn't have worn shorts.

Ryan chuckled, extricated himself from his beanbag with the ease of a veteran and offered her a hand up. She took it, but gave him a frosty glare.

Angie's response to their refusal was anything but cool. "Oooh. That's too bad." She cooed. "It's peach-kiwi. I could really use some help in eating it."

"And we'd love to help you out." Jennie gripped Ryan's arm and steered him toward the door. "Unfortunately, Ryan is allergic to fruit—" She'd nearly said *fruitcakes like you*, but didn't. Angie may have been an outrageous flirt, but she was also Cathy's friend and had given them what Jennie hoped would be a solid lead.

They thanked Angie for her help and left a phone number. "Call me if you think of anything that might help us find Cathy and the kids," Jennie added, wanting to remind her why they'd come.

Angie promised she would.

"Allergic to fruit?" Ryan hung an arm across Jennie's shoulders. "Couldn't you have come up with a better excuse than that?"

Jennie shrugged away. "I didn't see you making any. If I hadn't insisted on leaving, we—make that you—would probably be sitting back there letting her spoon-feed you."

For some reason Ryan found that extremely funny.

Jennie strode out ahead of him. She'd gone half a block when Ryan grabbed Jennie's arm and swung her around. "I know you're mad at me. I can almost see the steam coming out of your ears. What did I do?"

"You don't know? Ryan, I have never seen such blatant display of flirting in my life. She was all over you. And you encouraged her."

"Encouraged her? I just sat there. What did you want me to do, slap her hands? We were trying to get information that might help us find your brother."

Jennie winced, but didn't back down. Instead she hooked her arm around Ryan's, snuggled close, and fluttered her eyelashes. "I'm right-brained," she mimicked in a breathy voice. She let go of Ryan's arm and stuffed her hands in her shorts pockets. "If you ask me she's a no-brain."

Ryan grinned. "You're jealous."

"Am not."

He jogged ahead of her, turned around, and

blocked her path. "You are too. Hey, I'm not complaining. I'm flattered."

Jennie pushed him aside and kept walking. A smile tugged at the corners of her mouth. "I'm not jealous." *At least not anymore.*

Jennie stopped walking, suddenly shifting her attention back to Cathy Williams and her connection with Nick's disappearance. "Anyway, you're right. I need to be concentrating on Nick." Even as she said it, she realized that something had changed inside her. Her mind had somehow walled up the searing pain and flood of emotions connected with Nick's disappearance and left her heart numb.

Gram had explained the phenomenon once after Grandpa Ian had been killed in the bombing while he was on assignment in the Middle East. When people asked her how she coped, Gram would say, "I think the Lord has given me a pain killer. Just enough to ease the pain and numb the heart. Otherwise it would be unbearable."

That's what had happened. God had given her something to numb the pain and to help her focus on finding Nick, rather than caving in to the grief of losing him. It even allowed her to think about other things—like Ryan, but more important, it allowed her to think more objectively where Nick was concerned.

Ryan settled his arm back around Jennie. This time she left it there, drawing comfort from his presence. "You're right about something else too," Jennie said after they'd walked a few feet. She glanced into his blue eyes and offered what she hoped would be an apologetic smile. "I was jealous."

He dropped a light kiss on her nose. "You don't

have to be, you know. I haven't even thought of being with another girl since the first time I kissed you."

Which is more than you can say for yourself, McGrady. As if to drive home the point, her conscience brought to mind three guys she had developed a profound liking for . . . Scott Chambers, the hot-headed environmentalist she'd met in Florida. The thought of Scott working so hard to save the dolphins still warmed her. In some ways she thought he went to extremes to protect the environment, but she admired him for taking a stand.

Then there was Rocky, her favorite cop. Jennie would never forget how he risked his job and his life to protect her and Allison from a determined killer. His caring went above and beyond the call of duty. Not in a romantic way, she reminded herself. He was more like the older brother she never had. A kindred spirit.

And Dominic, from Bogota, Columbia. Even though he'd nearly gotten her killed, those chocolate brown eyes, charm, and intensity still singed her heart. The Caribbean cruise, the moonlit nights. Under different circumstances . . .

No, she erected a mental roadblock. They were friends. End of story. So why did it all seem so confusing? Why did she feel such strong ties to each one of them? *You are such a hypocrite, McGrady. You criticize Lisa for falling in love with every guy she meets. You may not be falling in love, but the attraction is sure there.*

Unable to argue the point, Jennie glanced at Ryan from the sidewalk lines she'd been trying not to step on, and realized he was waiting for an answer. What was it he'd said? Oh yes. He hadn't thought about other girls. Jennie smiled at the response that came to mind.

She could have said "me too" without lying. After all, she hadn't thought about other girls either.

She ignored her weird sense of humor, opting to keep her mouth shut, and hoped her smile would suffice. Actually, Jennie didn't know what to say. Only a month ago, she thought Ryan was the only guy she could ever love. This boy-girl thing sure could be confusing.

"It's okay, Jennie." Ryan removed his arm from her shoulder and reached for her hand.

"What's okay?"

"That you've dated other guys."

"I didn't say . . ."

"You didn't have to. I can read it in your eyes." He squeezed her hand. "Anyway. It's my fault. I should have told you how I felt before I left. Truth is, I wasn't sure until I got out there on that fishing boat. I missed you so much—"

"I missed you too."

"Hey, listen," Ryan said. "I have an idea. How about when this is all over and we find Nick, I take you out on a real date. We'll have dinner and go to a movie."

Jennie thought that was the most wonderful idea she'd ever heard and told him so. *You're a lucky woman, McGrady,* she reminded herself. Guys like Ryan don't come along very often. He's unbelievably understanding. *Maybe a little too understanding.* The critical thought had come from somewhere deep inside, emerging like an ember and bursting into flames. Jennie snuffed it out before it could spread. Ridiculous. Unfounded. Absurd.

They met Gram and J.B. in front of the library and

compared notes, then decided to check out Cathy's boyfriend before heading home. While they weren't able to talk to him personally, they did learn from a housemate that Judson had not returned to his dorm the night Cathy had stood him up—the same night Cathy and the children had disappeared.

After calling the police with their findings, they ate lunch and headed home. Gram and J.B. both cautioned Jennie not to get her hopes up, but it didn't do any good. She was certain Judson would lead them to Nick. She also felt sure that the police would find Nick, Hannah, and Cathy alive. Judson, after all, was a law student, not a killer. Maybe he and Cathy had gone somewhere and taken the kids with them.

But why? An errant voice in her head argued. *What reason would he have to take the kids? Cathy maybe, but not the kids. Since Cathy was baby-sitting, she may have insisted on taking Hannah, but certainly not Nick. And what about Bernie? And Nick's shirt* . . . Jennie didn't have any answers. She tried to put herself in Judson's place and after a while gave up. None of it made sense. But then crime seldom did.

15

When they arrived back at the house, Mom ran out to meet them. "They've picked up a suspect," she said. "The young man Cathy was dating. The police think he may have abducted them. He fits the description of the man in Washington Park."

"Did they find Nick?" Jennie asked hopefully.

"Not yet."

"With any luck, we'll have a confession by day's end." Concern and relief mingled in J.B.'s blue-gray eyes. With his accent—a mix of Irish brogue and British upper class—and his sophisticated charm, he reminded Jennie of another J.B.—James Bond. Somehow the thought buoyed her.

J.B. left, saying he had some important business to take care of at work. Gram asked him to drop her off at the police station.

When they'd gone, Mom shifted her attention to Jennie. "By the way, that boy across the street. Doug. The police released him. Apparently they couldn't find anything to charge him with."

"Have you seen him?" Jennie asked, relieved that her suspicions about Doug were unfounded. She'd almost forgotten about him. Now that they had a more likely suspect, she chided herself for being so quick to blame him.

"No," Mom answered, "but his mother came over to see how the search for Cathy and the kids was going. Seems like a really nice person. I hope for her sake that Doug is able to stay out of trouble."

Jennie hoped so too. "I'll bet this Judson guy's the one we're after," she said, voicing her earlier thoughts aloud. Now all that remained was to wait until the police questioned their suspect and gathered the evidence. Judson would soon confess and Nick would be home by bedtime.

Only it didn't happen that way. At 10:30 Jennie was still waiting. Lisa and her family had gone home earlier in the day after Lisa started running a fever. Gram and J.B. hadn't come back and Mom had fallen asleep on the couch.

"Jennie, will you sit down?" Ryan's voice broke through her deliberations.

"What?" She stared at him, then realized she'd been pacing. He patted an empty space beside him on the porch swing. "Sit. You're making me nervous."

She settled beside him and leaned her head on his shoulder. After a couple of minutes, she bounced back up. "I can't." She began to pace again. "I'm just too . . . I don't know . . . wound up. Why haven't they called? They can't still be questioning this Judson guy. It's making me crazy."

Ryan stopped the chair's swinging motion and got up. "Look, if you have to move around, let's go for a walk."

Without giving him an answer, Jennie raced down

the steps and across the lawn. He caught up to her on the sidewalk and grabbed her hand. Even the short jaunt had relaxed her some.

"So tell me about your summer," he said. "Sounds like you've had a pretty busy one so far."

Ryan was trying to get Jennie's mind off the case and she appreciated his efforts. She told him about the trips she'd taken and the mysteries she'd helped to solve.

"So what about your dad?" Ryan asked. "I thought your big goal this summer was to find him. Have you given up on it?"

Jennie hesitated, again grateful for the diversion, but not sure how much to tell him. "It was. I had to give it up. Government orders."

"And you did? Somehow, that doesn't sound like you."

"I didn't—not at first. I decided to take matters into my own hands and go on television. Big mistake. I had the FBI and the DEA down on me the minute it aired. They told us Dad had been working on a top-secret drug case when his plane went down and—well, to make a long story short, Dad won't be coming back."

"So he really did die in the plane crash?"

"The government has declared him legally dead." Jennie twisted the end of her braid around her finger. More than anything she wanted to tell the truth, but couldn't. Jennie needed to change the subject before she confided too much. "So, tell me about Alaska."

Ryan shrugged. "Not much to tell. Fishing's great. Unfortunately, it gets old really fast. We stay out about a week at a time. When we dock, the guys go nuts.

Most of them spend their time boozing it up. I call my folks, and you when you're home. I pick up supplies, then go stay with some friends I met up there. Dick and Sandy Harris. They run a homeless shelter. I usually help them while I'm in town. They feed me and give me a place to sleep in return."

"Sounds kind of lonely."

"It is. I wish I didn't have to go back."

"You're going back? This summer?" Disappointment settled in on her like a heavy fog.

"Have to. I signed a contract. They let me come home for a couple weeks. I told them I had a family emergency. I know you're not real family, but I wanted to be with you."

How could she even have considered liking other guys? Ryan was perfect—thoughtful, logical, intelligent. Everything a girl could want.

They'd circled two blocks and were crossing Magnolia Street when the Stuarts' front door opened.

"Chuck, don't," Anne screamed.

"This is all your fault," Chuck shouted back through the door. "You should have left her with the McGrady kid. If anything happens to Hannah as a result of that fool sister of yours, I swear I'll kill you."

He spun around and walked toward their blue van, his jaw rigid with anger. If he'd seen Jennie and Ryan, he didn't acknowledge the fact. He slammed the door, started the van, and burned rubber as he tore out of the driveway.

Anne stood in the doorway, her hand over her mouth. She was crying. She seemed frightened, and after witnessing Chuck's hostility Jennie could understand why. When Anne saw Ryan and Jennie, she let out a sharp cry, sounding like a wounded animal, then closed the door.

"I'm going to talk to her," Jennie said, starting for the house.

"Wait." Ryan grabbed her arm and pulled her back. "I don't think this would be a good time."

"Ryan, she's scared. Her daughter and sister are missing. She has to be heartbroken and that . . . that jerk of a husband is blaming her."

"I still don't think it's a good idea. She didn't act like she wanted company."

"She's embarrassed and hurt. I don't blame her for not wanting to see anyone. But she needs help." Jennie pulled out of Ryan's grasp and headed across the lawn to the front door. After two rings, Anne opened the door.

She kept her head down and slightly at an angle, but that didn't hide the puffy eyes, the large red slap mark on her cheek, and an already swollen lip.

"He hit you!" Jennie stared at Anne in disbelief. She'd heard about men who battered their wives, but had never dreamed that Chuck Stuart could be one of them.

Anne raised her hand and tentatively touched her swelling mouth. "This? It's nothing. I . . . ran into the door."

"Why are you protecting him? You should call the police."

"No. I told you he didn't do this."

"I saw how angry he was. You were arguing and . . ."

"He's terribly upset about Hannah. You of all people should understand." Anne glanced away, refusing to meet Jennie's eyes. "Besides, Chuck is right. This whole thing is my fault. I never should have left Hannah with Cathy."

"That doesn't give him the right to hit you," Jennie argued.

"He didn't."

"But the police can help . . ."

"No." Anne's pleading green eyes looked straight into Jennie's. "I know you want to help, but *please* don't get involved in this. If you call the police, I'll deny it."

Jennie glanced back at Ryan, who hadn't spoken during the entire encounter. He stood there with a shocked look on his face, probably wondering, like Jennie, how a guy who seemed so normal could beat up his own wife.

Jennie's gaze snapped back to Anne. A thought buried itself into her brain with the intensity of a bullet. "Has Mr. Stuart ever . . . um . . . hurt Hannah? I mean . . . would he . . ." Jennie paused for a moment, wondering how to ask the question burning in her mind. *Just say it, McGrady. Tell her.* She opened her mouth to try again, but Anne stopped her.

"I know what you're thinking, Jennie." Anne's voice had taken on a hostile tone. "Chuck would never hurt Hannah, or Nick for that matter. He certainly didn't have anything to do with their disappearance. We were gone, remember?" Anne closed the door, abruptly cutting off any more conversation.

What she couldn't close as easily was Jennie's imagination. "Come on," Jennie said, turning to go. "If she won't tell the police, I will."

Ryan followed her down the stairs and out onto the

sidewalk. "Do you really think Chuck had something to do with Hannah and Nick's disappearance? Like Anne said, they were gone. Judson seems a more likely prospect."

Jennie lifted her shoulders in a shrug. "Chuck may have had an alibi, but he might also have had an accomplice. He could have paid someone to abduct Hannah."

"Why would he do that? And even if he did, why take Nick and Cathy?"

"I don't know. Maybe he's planning to divorce Anne and wanted to make sure he gets the kid. Maybe he only meant for whoever did it to take Hannah, but Cathy and Nick got in the way."

"You're reaching on this one, Jennie. Stuart may be a hot-headed jerk, but do you honestly think he'd kidnap his own daughter? What would be the point?"

"You're right. I don't know why I even considered it. Maybe I just wanted another suspect in case Judson doesn't—" Jennie left her sentence dangling as a patrol car pulled up. Rocky got out and came toward them.

"Hi," Jennie greeted. "You have great timing. I was just going to call you."

"We aim to please. Thought I'd come by on my way home from work and check things out." He looked from Jennie to Ryan, then held out a hand. "Name's Rockford. You are?"

"Ryan Johnson. I'm a friend of the family." Jennie waited for him to tell Rocky he was her boyfriend. He didn't. Fine. If he only wanted to be known as a family friend, she could accept that. Or not.

"A little late for you two to be out, isn't it?" Rocky asked.

Annoyed at his arrogance and Ryan's indifference, Jennie glanced at her watch. 11:15. "Actually, I've been waiting for you. You were going to let us know about Judson. What took you so long? Is he . . ."

Rocky sighed and shook his head. "We had to release him. Seems he headed out this way, but changed his mind and went to Salem to see his folks instead."

"And you believed him?" Jennie clung to the slender thread of hope that the ordeal would be over with Judson's arrest.

"Them. His folks verified him being there about the time you said you last saw Nick. He's still a person of interest. Parents have been known to lie to protect their kids."

"So have wives," Jennie muttered, her mood disintegrating by the second.

16

Rocky lifted an eyebrow. "You find something I should know about?"

Jennie described Chuck Stuart's angry departure and Anne's denial that he'd hit her. After hearing her report, Rocky whistled. "Changes the picture some, I'd say. Looks like we'd better do a little more intensive questioning. These domestic violence cases can be pretty tricky."

After mumbling about how much he hated DVs, Rocky left. Jennie and Ryan returned to the house. "Looks like everyone's gone to bed," Ryan said as he opened the door and stepped aside to let Jennie in.

Jennie didn't answer.

"Ah . . . look, I get the feeling you're upset with me again. What did I do this time?"

She was tempted to say "nothing," but that would have been a lie. Not that she was above telling one, but at the moment she felt confrontational and irritated and . . . just plain obstinate. Ryan ran a hand through his blond hair, pushing an errant lock off his forehead. Ordinarily Jennie would have found the action cute and him adorable, but not tonight.

"It's not what you did, Ryan," she finally answered. "It's what you didn't say. Earlier today you gave me the impression we were going together. Just now—out there with Rocky, you referred to yourself as a friend of the family. I guess I'd just like to know why you didn't tell Rocky you were my boyfriend. Or at least *my* friend."

Ryan shrugged. "I was waiting for you to say something. I mean—the way you looked at each other I thought maybe you and he . . ."

"Had something going? Why does everyone think that?" Jennie planted her feet apart and folded her arms—probably to keep from hitting him. "In case you hadn't noticed, he's old enough to be my—" Jennie let her arms drop and gave him an exasperated look. "I was under the impression you cared about me."

"I do."

"Do you? If I told you right this minute that I was madly in love with Rocky, what would you do?"

Ryan frowned. "Are you?"

The sound that came out of Jennie's mouth sounded like a cross between a growl and a groan. "No. But that's not the point." Jennie hauled in a deep breath and let it out to the count of five. "Never mind," she said at last. "I'm sorry I said anything."

"Jennie . . ." Ryan cupped her shoulders with his hands and pulled her toward him and kissed her forehead. "I know what you mean. You want to know where I stand. You're wondering why I didn't tell Robo-cop to get lost."

"Robo-cop?"

Ryan grinned. "Okay, Rocky. Anyway, if you chose him over me, I'd walk away."

Jennie opened her mouth to protest.

"I'd walk away. But that doesn't mean I wouldn't be hurt—or upset. I don't want to lose you, Jen. We've been friends a long time. I can even see us getting married someday, but I can't make that kind of commitment now. Like I said before, we've both got a lot of years of school to get through."

"I know. And I really am sorry for getting mad at you. I had this idea that seeing you again would clear everything up for me, but it hasn't. If anything, I'm more confused."

He planted a kiss on her nose. "Me too. Being tired and having Nick gone sure doesn't help. I think it would be better if we didn't try to deal with our relationship right now. Let's talk about us after we find Nick and Hannah."

Jennie looked into his clear blue eyes. Next to Lisa, Ryan was her best friend. He'd come all the way from Alaska to help her find Nick—to offer her family comfort during the ordeal.

"Why don't you try to get some sleep," he said. "Maybe by morning the police will have some real answers."

Jennie doubted it, but took his advice anyway. At least she tried to. She tossed around like a Mexican jumping bean most of the night. Her mind kept bouncing around from suspect to suspect, picking up random thoughts and tossing them out again. Who had run down Bernie? Had the same person taken Nick, Hannah, and Cathy? Had it been a random crime, committed by some creep who got cheap thrills from ruining other peoples' lives? Or had it been someone wanting to get even? Doug? Judson? Chuck Stuart, or maybe even Anne? Though Gram had assured her otherwise, the possibility still existed that one of Dad's enemies had abducted Nick. That possibility seemed less likely now. It didn't do much good to take a hostage if you didn't let anyone know about it.

All of her ruminating did little to solve the crime, but it did add another suspect—Anne Stuart. Sometime during the night Jennie had come up with the notion that Anne may have arranged for Cathy to take Hannah. Not long ago, Jennie had read about a mother who had abducted her daughter to protect the child from an abusive father. The woman had gone to jail because she refused to reveal the child's whereabouts. Jennie tried to imagine what it would be like living with an abusive husband or father. She'd want to get out, that's for sure. It seemed the most plausible explanation, except for one thing. If Anne had wanted to move Hannah to a safe place, why take Nick?

———

Thursday morning when she came down for breakfast, Officer Beck was sitting at the kitchen table with Gram and J.B. Jennie eased a chair out and sat down.

He glanced at Jennie, nodded, then went on talking to Mom. "I know this is difficult for you, Mrs. McGrady, but we have to explore every avenue. Most of the time in a case like this when none of our outside leads pan out, we have to start looking at the people closest to the victims."

Mom set a cup of coffee in front of him, than sat down. "I realize that," she said, "but Michael would never be involved with something like this."

Jennie almost dropped the milk she'd just poured.

"Michael? You suspect Michael?"

He ignored Jennie and continued his conversation with Mom. "You did break off your engagement with him."

"Yes, but Michael loves Nick."

"My point exactly. Did he love the kid enough to abduct him? We see custody battles like this all the time, where the husband or wife takes off with the kids. I know you weren't married, but the possibility exists."

"I agree with Mom," Jennie said. "Michael loves Nick, but he loves Mom and me too. If you're checking out this custody thing as a motive, you might have more luck with the Stuarts." Jennie capsulized the scene she and Ryan had witnessed the night before, ending with her misgivings about both Chuck and Anne Stuart.

Beck wrote it all down and promised to look into it. "At this point," he went on, "we aren't ruling anyone out—especially not family. Which means that over the next few days we'll be doing a thorough investigation of each one of you."

"Wait a minute," Jennie demanded. "Are you saying you think my mother—and me? I can't believe you're wasting time even considering us."

Beck ran a hand across his balding head and let out an exasperated sigh. "A woman recently murdered her children because they were too much of a burden. A teenaged boy drowned his two-year-old sister in the bathtub because she wouldn't quit crying. I could go on and on. You seem like a nice enough kid, but so did those people. I've been in the business long enough to know that we can't take anything for granted. We turn over every rock we can find and hope to heaven we find the right answers before the brass decides to deep six the case in the unsolved bin."

Beck drained his cup and set it back down. "Which will happen if I don't get back to work. Sometime today, Mrs. McGrady, I'd like you and your daughter to come downtown to take a lie detector test. You'll be questioned at the same time."

After he'd gone Jennie picked at her blueberry pancakes, but couldn't manage to actually take a bite. "How could he suspect any of us?"

"I know it sounds cruel, luv," J.B. said as he reached for the syrup, "but it's necessary."

"Unfortunately, he's right," Gram agreed. "The perpetrator is often a family member or acquaintance. When a child disappears, more often than not, one of the parents is involved."

J.B. took a bite of pancake, then chased it down with a sip of coffee. "Beck is being objective—looking into every possibility."

Jennie wished she could be more objective as well, but spending precious time questioning the wrong people didn't make much sense.

After breakfast Gram and J.B. promised to accompany Mom to the station. When they excused themselves to shower and get dressed, Jennie opted to do the dishes. She'd go later. Maybe.

Ryan sauntered in as the others were leaving and Jennie fixed him a plate of pancakes, bacon, and scrambled eggs.

While he ate, she told him about the police wanting to interrogate her family. "Do you want to come down to the police station with me? The thought of going through a lie detector test has me scared to death. I mean, what if I'm so nervous it says I'm lying when I'm not?"

"It won't, Jen. You'll do okay." He took a couple bites of bacon, "Ummm . . . I'd like to go with you, but I really have to go home for a few hours today. I need some fresh clothes and Mom is laying a guilt trip on me. I've only talked to her for a few minutes on the phone since I got back. Maybe I could borrow your car, drive down this morning, and come back later tonight. I was going to ask you to come with me, but since you have to go—"

"I'd love to go with you. There's no reason I can't go in and do the stupid test tomorrow." Home for Ryan was in Bay Village next door to Gram. A trip to the beach sounded far better than a trip to the police station.

She'd expected an argument from Mom and Gram about putting off the interrogation, but didn't get it. Gram thought a few hours at the beach sounded like a wonderful idea and asked Jennie to pick up her mail and check the house while she was there.

On the two hour drive down, Jennie and Ryan talked again about the various suspects and set up dozens of scenarios. She had asked Ryan to drive the Mustang while she took notes. Much as she'd done the night before, Jennie set up the players, writing each name down, listing their opportunities, motives, and whereabouts.

"I think I can pretty well eliminate Doug," Jennie said, scratching his name off the list. "He was interviewing for that job at Hammond's Construction, and has been working every day since."

"What about Judson?"

Jennie chewed on the end of her pencil. "I'm leaving him on the list. He could have swung by the Stuarts', picked up Cathy and the kids, and stashed them somewhere between Portland and Salem—or even taken them to Salem. Like Rocky said, parents have been known to lie for their kids."

"Yeah, especially if they're suspect in a case like this." Ryan glanced at her, then back at the road. "Who else is on your list?"

"I keep coming back to the Stuarts."

"But they were both gone."

"What if Anne and Cathy worked it out ahead of time? What if Cathy took the kids and is keeping them in a safe place until all this blows over?"

"Okay, that makes sense. Cathy takes Hannah, hides out until Anne can get away, but that doesn't explain Nick or Bernie. Have you considered the possibility that we're dealing with two different incidents? Cathy could have taken Hannah somewhere. She probably sent Nick home, only something happened before he got there."

Jennie shuddered. Somehow it had seemed safer to connect him to Cathy and Hannah.

"You have to admit it makes more sense," Ryan went on. "Let's say it happened that way. Cathy told Nick to go home. She's hiding out somewhere right now with Hannah. They're out of the picture. So what happened to Nick? We know Bernie got hit by a car. Nick would go after him, right?"

Jennie couldn't answer. Even though she fought against it, the images of Bernie's bloodied fur and Nick's Mickey Mouse shirt hammered their way into her mind. She felt as if someone had reached inside her chest and yanked out her heart. So much for God numbing the pain. Jennie didn't know what had opened the flood gates, but a wave of agony crashed through her. Tears spilled from her tightly closed eyelids. A sob tore itself away from her reserve. She was losing control and she had no idea how to stop it.

17

Ryan reached for her hand and held it. "I'm sorry."

Jennie shook her head. "Not . . . your . . . fault," she managed to say.

The car slowed as Ryan pulled into a turnout. He retrieved a box of tissues from the backseat, handed her a few, and wrapped his arms around her. Everything broke loose inside and Jennie crumbled.

When the crying finally stopped, she drew in a long shuddering breath and withdrew from Ryan's arms. The tears in his eyes almost started her crying again. She scrubbed her eyes against her palms and blew her nose. "I'm sorry."

"You don't need to be."

"I got your shirt all wet."

"It's okay. It needed washing anyway." He squeezed her hand. "Feel better?"

She nodded. Strangely, she did feel better. Embarrassed, but better. "We should get going before your mother thinks *we've* disappeared."

"I feel so bad about this, Jen. I just wish there was something more I could do."

"Me too. I mean, that I could do." An idea rose and

broke through her grief like a colorful balloon. She grasped Ryan's arm. "I can't believe I didn't think of it before. Gram says nothing ever happens without a reason."

"What are you talking about?" Ryan rebuckled his seat belt and merged into the highway.

"We thought we were coming down to the beach to see your mom and get your stuff, right?"

"That was the plan."

"I think there's another reason for our being here."

"Which is?" Ryan cast her an I-think-you're-losing-it look.

"We're going to visit Anne and Cathy's parents."

"The Williams? Why?"

"I'm not sure. I'd like to ask them some questions. Maybe they've heard from Cathy. Who knows? If Cathy did take Hannah she may be there. She might even have Nick."

"They're nice people, Jen. They wouldn't dream of breaking the law."

"You're probably right, but it still wouldn't hurt to stop."

"Okay, we'll stop. I'll have to call Mom from Lincoln City and let her know we'll be late."

For the rest of the way to the Williams' Bed & Breakfast, Jennie imagined a dozen different scenarios. She'd drive up and find the children playing in the yard. In another she and Ryan would sneak in after nightfall and peer into every room. Though the scenes differed, they all ended happily, with Nick spotting her and flying into her arms.

Darker, more sinister endings hung on the periphery of her mind, but Jennie refused to let them in. She had to think positively.

———————

Mr. and Mrs. Williams, though surprised by their visit, were much warmer and friendlier than Jennie expected. She'd hoped to catch them red-handed. Doing what, Jennie wasn't sure.

When they pulled into the driveway, Mr. Williams emerged from one of the many out buildings. He wiped his hands on a rag and apologized for smelling of turpentine. He'd been refinishing a solid oak table from the stash of furniture heaped in their antique store. The store had once been a carriage house and made an excellent place for guests to browse. Following Mr. Williams in, they found Mrs. Williams in the restored 1890 mansion, baking bread, which she'd be serving to their guests at the evening meal.

"Jennie. Ryan." She pushed a lock of her nearly white hair off her forehead. "What a pleasant surprise. I do wish it were under better circumstances." Her cheeks were red and flushed from the kitchen's heat, reminding Jennie of Mom's ceramic figurine of Mrs. Santa Claus. "Bob," she turned to her husband. "Why don't you show our guests into the parlor? I'll fix some ice tea and cookies and I'll be right in."

While Mrs. Williams may have resembled Mrs. Claus, Mr. Williams bore little resemblance to Santa, except maybe in body type. Stern, strict, Jennie could see him as the type of parent who'd spank first and ask questions later.

Bob excused himself to clean up, leaving Jennie and Ryan alone. The parlor, along with the rest of the house, was classic Victorian. They'd restored the place as closely as possible to its original glory. The home had been a former senator's vacation home. Although Jennie hadn't stayed there, she'd read the brochure and visited a couple of times with Gram. The ten thousand square foot house now accommodated up to thirty guests comfortably. *Plenty of room to hide a college student and two small children,* Jennie thought.

"I'm so glad you've come. Anne has been keeping me informed and I watch every newscast, but it's good to have someone here in person. Have you heard anything?"

"I'm afraid not." Jennie accepted the ice tea and selected a chocolate chip cookie from a sculptured pink plate. "Thanks."

The older woman sighed, offering the same to Ryan. "The sheriff came by this morning. He said they're questioning everyone in both families. He even searched the inn and the grounds. Imagine thinking we'd have anything to do with taking those poor children. It's inconceivable." She shook her head. "Still, I suppose they need to ask, what with all the strange goings-on these days." Clasping her hands together, she closed her eyes to fight back her tears. "I'm sorry. Hannah is our only grandchild. And Cathy . . . It's so hard not knowing."

Jennie shoved her ideas of the Williams being involved in a conspiracy with Anne and Cathy out of her head. If the sisters had taken Hannah—and Nick—Jennie doubted that Bob and Emily Williams knew about it.

"Mrs. Williams," Jennie began, "did Anne ever

mention that she and Chuck were having marital problems?"

The older woman frowned. "Now why would you ask that? You don't think Chuck—" She left the sentence dangling.

"Last night Chuck and Anne were having an argument. I'm sure he hit her. She denied it, but it makes me wonder." Jennie also wondered why Emily Williams was so quick to raise the question of Chuck's guilt.

"Chuck Stuart is a fool," Bob answered gruffly as he entered the room. He strode toward them and sat on a frail-looking velvet loveseat with ornately curved legs. Jennie expected the couch to crumble under his weight. It didn't. "Never did like that boy."

"Bob!" Emily chided, apparently chafing at the thought of having their family problems aired.

"Well, it's true, Emily. We should never have let her marry him. I tried to warn her." Bob glanced from his wife to Jennie and pinched his lips together.

"As if we could have stopped her." Emily shifted in her chair so she faced Jennie more fully. "We've been concerned for a long time, Jennie. About a month ago, Anne told us she planned to end the marriage. Their trip to the coast was an attempt to work things out."

"If you ask me, Chuck is behind this whole thing," Bob said. "I wouldn't put it past him to swipe Hannah in order to get back at Anne—to hurt all of us for that matter. Though, why he'd take your little brother is beyond me."

It was beyond Jennie too. She'd come suspecting Anne and Cathy, but after talking to the Williams, Jennie was just as confused as ever. They said their goodbyes to the older couple and continued their drive down the coast. Jennie pulled her shoulder strap forward and let it snap back. Nick, Cathy, and Hannah had vanished and Jennie had no idea what to do about it. *Face it, McGrady,* she told herself. *You don't have what it takes to be a detective. You don't even know where to begin.*

More than anything in the world, she wanted to find Nick, and of course Hannah and Cathy. The only problem was, in order to solve a problem, a person had to think about all the possibilities. Jennie didn't want to do that. Thinking about what could have happened to Nick was just too painful. She shared her frustrations with Ryan. "It might be better if I just let it go. The police know what they're doing. It's hard to admit it, but maybe I should stop trying to investigate. Every time I do something, the police have already been there."

"You're worrying me, Jen. I've never known you to give up on anything." When Jennie didn't answer, he reached over and held her hand. "Why don't we just try to relax for the rest of the day. We'll walk on the beach, have dinner with my mom and dad, then drive back to Portland. Maybe tomorrow things will seem a little better."

Jennie squeezed his hand. "Maybe."

———

Around five o'clock, they pulled into Ryan's driveway in Bay Village. Mrs. Johnson ran out of the house and hugged them both. One of the hardest things about a crisis, Jennie decided, was trying not to fall apart when people told you how concerned they were and how they'd been praying. Ryan's mother did all of that, then wanted to know how everyone was doing. While Ryan excused himself to do some laundry and repack, Jennie dutifully gave her a report on the rest of the family.

"Your grandmother is a sly one," Mrs. Johnson said. "We didn't have a clue she was planning a wedding."

"Actually, we didn't either," Jennie admitted. "It was a spur of the moment thing. J.B. just hustled her off to Europe and proposed."

"I only got to meet him briefly, but he seemed like a nice man. Helen said he works for the FBI."

Jennie nodded.

"I have to tell you, hon, I've been worried about Helen doing all that traveling alone. Having a husband around will be a steadying influence on her, don't you think?"

Steadying influence? J.B.? In his line of work? Jennie doubted it, but didn't say so. When Ryan came in, Jennie seized the opportunity to escape. It wasn't that she didn't like Mrs. Johnson, but at the moment, she couldn't tolerate any more chatting. Besides, it seemed like a good idea to give Ryan and his mom a chance to be alone together.

Using the key Gram had left with the Johnsons, Jennie crossed the lawns and let herself into Gram's house. She hadn't been there in over a month. Memories of Gram's disappearance and the missing diamonds assaulted her. They'd gone through some pretty frightening moments.

But you made it, McGrady. That's the important thing. Maybe you didn't have all the answers, but you didn't give up. She sank into an oversized chair in front of the picture window that offered a view of the ocean. After staring at the waves for several minutes, she began to pray, but after a few minutes just sat in silence watching the waves crash against the rocks. Jennie had received no answers, but she did feel reassured and strangely at peace. Whatever happened she'd handle it. But that was before she got the phone call.

She picked up the receiver on the first ring.

"Jennie? Thank God I caught you." The tension in Gram's voice reached through the wires and wrapped itself around her chest like tentacles of an invisible monster. "Gram?" Jennie gasped. "What's wrong?"

18

"Is Ryan there with you?" Gram asked.

"No . . . why?" She'd no sooner gotten the words out when Ryan opened the door and walked in.

"Has she told you yet?" Ryan closed the door and walked toward her.

Jennie stared at him, moving her head from side to side. He lowered himself onto the arm of the chair and took hold of her free hand. Jennie gripped it and pressed the phone to her ear so hard it hurt. "He's here," she told Gram. The news would have to be pretty bad if Gram felt Jennie needed someone with her. Jennie took a deep breath and steeled herself to hear it.

"We think we have a pretty good idea of what happened." Gram paused and cleared her throat.

Jennie felt like a volcano ready to erupt. "Gram, please. Whatever it is, just tell me."

"I'm trying, Jennie. It's so hard on the phone." She hesitated again.

"Gram?"

"Jennie." The voice no longer belonged to Gram, but to J.B. "I'm afraid your gram isn't up to tellin' you

142

just now, lass. So the job falls to me. We've learned some things about the case and wanted you to know before you heard it on the news."

"What . . . what is it?" Jennie stammered. If Gram was so upset she couldn't even talk, the news must be worse than she had thought.

"We have a witness who saw Cathy leave the Stuarts' house around six."

"He's just now coming forward?"

"Seems he's been out of town on business. He saw a picture of Cathy on a national news program this morning and recognized her. Last Monday, he'd been on his way to the airport and was driving down Magnolia Street when a woman he's certain was Cathy backed out of the Stuarts' driveway. Nearly ran him down. Seemed to be in quite a rush. She was driving Mrs. Stuart's tan Honda."

"What about the kids? Did he see them?"

"No. But we're fairly certain she had them along. Bernie was chasing after the car."

And he wouldn't have been doing that unless Nick was in it, Jennie finished the thought.

"Trouble is," J.B. went on, "we don't know what happened afterward."

"Did he see who hit Bernie?"

"Claims not."

While Cathy's actions didn't make sense, they confirmed Jennie's hopes that Nick might still be alive. So why had Gram been so upset? "That's good news, isn't it? I mean, that Cathy took the kids?"

"That's only part of the story, lass. I felt you should have some of the background." He paused, then in a voice almost as shaky as Gram's had been, added,

"Sheriff up in Lincoln County found what they think was the Stuarts' car this afternoon, on a logging trail off Highway 18, between Portland and Lincoln City."

"What do you mean *think*? Couldn't they tell?" Jennie glanced up at Ryan and tightened her grip on his hand.

"The only thing they've been able to identify so far is a piece of a license plate that must have ripped off in the explosion. If anyone was in the car at the time, they couldn't have survived."

Jennie let the phone slip from her hand and felt it drop onto her lap. She stared out at the ocean again.

Somewhere in a distant corner of her mind she could hear Ryan talking. She had no idea what he'd said. He hung up the phone and turned toward her. "Jennie . . . I'm sorry."

She didn't answer. How could she? What could she say?

She waited for the tears to come; they didn't. Instead the numbness set in again. "I need to go home."

Ryan nodded and walked with her to the door. "I can be ready in about fifteen minutes."

As it turned out, they didn't leave until nearly nine. Mrs. Johnson insisted they eat dinner before going home. Jennie agreed, but only because Ryan hadn't eaten since breakfast. The steaks his mother barbecued were probably as good as Ryan said, but to Jennie they were as tasteless as chewing wax.

After getting last-minute instructions to drive carefully, Jennie backed her Mustang out of the driveway and started home. As they passed the Williams' Bed and Breakfast Jennie slowed the car. "I wonder if they know?"

"They probably do," Ryan said. "The police usually try to inform the family before they release information to the press. Do you want to stop?"

"Yes," Jennie said, pulling into a left-turn lane, then stopping for traffic. When the lanes were clear, she made a U-turn and headed back.

Jennie pulled into the B&B's small parking lot. Bob Williams drove in beside them, got out of his battered brown pickup, and braced his hands against Jennie's door before she could get out. "We heard about the car bombing," he said through the open window. "Bad business that. Appreciate your stopping by, but this isn't a good time. The Mrs. ain't taking it so good." He glanced at the house, then back to Jennie. "She's not up to having visitors."

"I understand," Jennie said. "I just wanted to ask . . ."

"No! No more questions," he said abruptly, then immediately apologized for his brisk tone. "We've all been through a lot, yourself included. We don't know anything more about this mess than you do. Now if you'll excuse me, I have guests to tend to." Mr. Williams headed across the parking area and up the broad white steps. He paused to talk to a woman sitting on one of the white wicker chairs lining the porch before disappearing inside.

"I guess stopping wasn't such a good idea," Ryan said.

Jennie started the car and shifted into reverse. "Guess not." She backed around, taking care not to sideswipe the blue van parked next to her. "I wonder if Anne is here. This looks like their van."

"Maybe she came down to be with her folks."

"Yeah. Probably." Jennie frowned. "Only thing is, Chuck took off in their van. You don't think they're back together?"

Ryan shrugged. "That would explain Mr. Williams' foul mood."

"True. Although I can't imagine going back to someone like that."

———

Neither Jennie nor Ryan spoke much on the way home. Ryan had dozed off, probably mesmerized by the rhythm of the windshield wipers. Jennie concentrated on keeping the car in the right lane on the winding, rain-slickened highway. It had started raining at about Lincoln City and worsened through the coastal mountain range.

Jennie ducked instinctively as a truck passed her on a downhill run. The road disappeared behind what could have passed for Niagara Falls. Her heart slammed against her chest. She held her breath and kept a steady hand on the wheel. Three trucks later, Jennie swore she'd never drive in the rain again. Which was a pretty stupid promise to make when you lived in Oregon.

Her windshield wipers had just recovered from the last truck's deluge when a vehicle approached her from behind. Its bright lights glared in the rearview mirror, blinding her. Jennie fiddled with the knob to tip the mirror up. "I can't believe it," she muttered.

"Did you say something?" Ryan stretched and yawned.

"This guy's right on my bumper. I don't understand why some people think they have to follow so close."

"Tap your brakes," Ryan suggested. "Maybe he'll back off. If not, there's a passing lane up ahead. He can get by you there."

When the road widened, Jennie stayed in the right lane. So did the tailgater. The lights dimmed. For a moment, she thought he was going to pass. But only for a moment.

Jennie felt the impact a split second after hearing the crash.

"What the . . ." Ryan snapped to attention and whipped around in the seat. "He hit you!"

She held tightly to the wheel, concentrating on keeping the car on the road.

"Either that guy is the world's worst driver or he did that on purpose." Ryan ran both hands through his hair. "Maybe you'd better pull over."

"I'm not sure that's a good idea. I mean what if it's a gang who wants us to stop so they can steal the car, or kill us?"

The driver backed off. Bright lights illuminated the inside of her car. Ryan glanced back again. "Looks like he's going to pass. He's . . ."

Ryan never got to finish his sentence. The driver of the other vehicle bore down on them again. The impact sent the Mustang skidding onto loose gravel. Its headlights reached deep into the fog as they left the road.

19

Jennie had often been told that when you were about to die, your entire life flashed before you. She'd been about to die a number of times lately, but had never gotten the "life events" film. What played through Jennie's mind were strange bits and pieces of memories that were about as useless as Canadian coins in an Oregon vending machine.

As her Mustang free-fell downward, a scene from *Chitty Chitty Bang Bang* stuck in her mind. As the theme song drifted through her head, Jennie wished she'd been driving the flying Chitty instead of a Mustang.

She hoped the insurance was paid up—on her life as well as on the car. Jennie tightened her grip on the steering wheel. Nothing to do now but ride it out. She just wished she could see. Then wished she couldn't. Even with a torrential downpour blurring the windshield, she could see them below—trees.

Jennie closed her eyes, pressed her body into the seat, and sucked in a deep breath, preparing herself for impact. And undoubtedly death.

Branches screeched and thumped against the car.

It was a little like going on a roller coaster and through a giant bristle-brush car wash at the same time—only ten times worse. The deafening noises must have only gone on for a few seconds, but it seemed like forever. The car finally jolted to a stop.

When Jennie shifted to unbuckle her seat belt, the car teetered, then started falling again. This time it went backward, landing on its rear end with a thud. Like a restless sleeper trying to find a comfortable position, the Mustang groaned and dropped forward again.

After a few minutes Jennie decided the ride had ended. She stared into the darkness, trying to orient herself. *Either you're alive, McGrady, or all the reports you've heard about heaven were highly exaggerated.*

"Th-that was some ride, wasn't it?" She held a hand to her throat, surprised she had a voice. "The trees must have broken our fall."

Ryan didn't answer. "Ryan?" The dim light cast by the dash gave his skin a bluish tint. Panic sliced through her again. It hadn't occurred to her that Ryan might not have survived. She switched on the dome light and unbuckled her seat belt, then grabbed his shoulder. "Ryan, can you hear me?"

Nothing. Jennie pressed two fingers against his throat. When she found a pulse, she let out the breath she'd been holding. "Come on, Ryan, talk to me."

When he still didn't respond, Jennie placed her head against his chest. Its rise and fall reassured her. He must have hit his head. She reached up to turn his face toward her so she could see more clearly. Her hand encountered something warm and sticky. Blood.

She yanked her hand back as if it had been burned.

Don't panic, McGrady. Ryan needs you. Jennie took several deep breaths. *Come on, Jennie,* a voice seemed to say. *You know what to do.* "Stop the bleeding," she said aloud. "Gotta find something—" Jennie crawled into the backseat, ripped open Ryan's overnight bag, and yanked out a white cotton T-shirt. Positioning herself behind him, she wrapped it around his head. The seat was still in the partially reclined position it had been in before the accident. *Accident?* Whatever had happened up on that highway had definitely not been an accident.

She had to stop the bleeding. Jennie pressed her hand against the wound. "God, please let him be all right." She rested her head beside his and whispered, "You'd better not die on me, Johnson. You promised me dinner and a movie when this is over."

When this is over. Jennie wondered if it ever would be. Whatever *it* was. Someone had abducted Nick. Had they come after her too? But why? "You're too close, McGrady," she answered her own question. Maybe Nick had been too close too. He may have seen something he shouldn't have.

Jennie started shaking. Probably shock. She fumbled around for their jackets. Finding them, she placed the heaviest one over Ryan and slipped into the lighter one. Now what? She should get out of the car and go for help. Maybe she should try to pull Ryan out too. She'd heard about cars exploding after a crash. She really didn't want to move Ryan unless she had to—especially not out into the rain.

Jennie crawled back into the front seat and forced open the door. The rain had let up and was now falling in a light mist. This she could handle. She touched

Ryan's arm. "I have to go out for a while. Stay here. I'll be back as soon as I can." She zipped up her jacket. With any luck she'd still have a flashlight tucked in the emergency kit in the trunk. She hesitated a moment before stepping outside. The dome light may have helped her see better in the car, but it intensified the darkness.

Her feet should have hit the ground. They didn't. A scream escaped her throat and hung in the air where she left her heart and her stomach on the way down. She wrapped her head in her arms to protect her face from the limbs that slashed against her. Even with the tree limbs breaking her fall, she landed hard. Her legs crumpled under her as though they were made of cardboard instead of muscle and bone.

Pain ripped through her right leg. She moaned and rolled over onto her side. Jennie gritted her teeth and sat up, fighting off the nausea and swirling darkness that threatened to engulf her. She took some deep breaths. *Don't panic, McGrady. You're okay.*

Looking up she could see the white Mustang, perched like an oversized Christmas ornament, in a what was probably a stand of half a dozen douglas firs.

When the searing pain in her leg simmered down to a dull ache in her ankle, Jennie got to her feet and began her trek toward the highway some one hundred fifty feet away. *You can make it, McGrady,* she told herself. "Yeah," she answered. "I just wish it wasn't straight up."

She'd gone only a few feet when she saw a bouncing flashlight beam and heard someone thrashing through the woods toward her. Had they come to finish her and Ryan off?

"Is anyone there?" a man's voice called. The thrashing stopped, but the beam kept bouncing until it found her.

Jennie must have looked as terrified as she felt because the person at the other end of the light said, "It's okay. I'm here to help." He aimed the light up and down her body. "I can't believe you made it out of that alive," he said. "Saw the whole thing."

"I . . . Ryan is still in the car—it's in the trees. Up there."

"We'll get him down, don't you worry. You just sit down here and rest." The man took a silver emergency blanket out of his pack and wrapped it around her. "I've always carried one of these in my first aid kit," he explained. "Never needed it until now. There." He secured the blanket. "I called in on my cellular. The paramedics and police should be here any minute."

She thanked him and thanked God for sending him.

———

The following day, Jennie woke up in a hospital bed. Minor injuries, her doctor had said. Major pain. The first face she saw when she opened her eyes was Rocky's. He was sitting in a chair beside the bed, studying some papers.

"Hi," she croaked. Her throat felt like sandpaper.

"It's about time you woke up." He grinned and set the papers beside him. "I sent your mother and Gram down to have some breakfast. They've been here all night. I promised to watch you until they got back."

"I hope you weren't watching too close—I must look terrible." Jennie ran a hand through her hair and came up with a piece of moss. She grimaced, partly because of the moss, partly because the action brought a spasm of pain to her arm and shoulder.

"You look fine for someone who tried to fight Mother Nature and lost."

"Very funny." Jennie tried to scoot up in bed, then gave it up. It hurt too much. "How's Ryan?" During the night, the paramedics had ambulanced them both to Emmanuel Hospital in Portland. Ryan had regained consciousness, but the doctor was concerned about his head injury.

"He's got a whopper of a headache." Rocky offered her a lopsided grin. "Says to tell you the date's still on." His expression sobered. "So how are you feeling?"

"Like I've been run over by a truck."

"You were run over by a truck." He glanced at his notes. "Unfortunately, that's about all the guy who witnessed it could tell us."

"Do you think this has anything to do with Nick's disappearance?"

The door opened before he could answer. Gram and Mom walked in. After letting them fuss over her for a few minutes, Jennie assured them she'd be fine and asked them to sit down.

"Have you told her?" Gram asked, shifting her gaze to Rocky.

Jennie glanced at Rocky accusingly. "Told me what?"

"We're fairly certain we know who did it."

Jennie couldn't even venture a guess. The only people, other than family, who knew they were at the beach were Ryan's mom and Mr. and Mrs. Williams. Somehow she couldn't see any of them running her off the road. She'd eliminated Anne as a suspect after hearing about the explosion. They were such violent acts, only one person came to mind. "Chuck Stuart? I saw a blue van in the Williams' parking lot. I wondered at the time . . ."

Rocky shook his head. "Not a bad guess. We haven't ruled him out and still plan to question him. But my money's on your other neighbor. This morning we issued a warrant for Doug Reed's arrest."

20

"Doug ran us off the road?" Jennie stared at him, refusing to believe that her new neighbor would try to kill her. "But he didn't even know I'd gone to the beach."

Rocky closed his notebook with a snap. "He could have followed you."

"Then why did he wait until we were coming back? The traffic wasn't that heavy going down. He had plenty of opportunities. Besides, he doesn't have a truck." *Why are you defending him, McGrady?* she asked herself. He'd seemed nice enough the last time they'd talked, but he could have been lulling her into a false sense of security.

"He could have stolen one."

Jennie frowned and sighed. "I suppose you have proof?"

"Enough. Reed didn't show up for work yesterday. His mother hasn't seen him since Tuesday night. The kid's on the run."

"I thought he had an alibi for when Nick disappeared. He was applying for a job."

"Yes, but Reed was one of a hundred applicants for

two positions. Truth is, no one at Hammond's can attest to the fact that he was actually there the whole time."

"What about the guy who saw Cathy leave with the kids? Doug wasn't with them."

"We're still working on that angle. Look, Jennie, we have evidence that links Reed to the crime."

"I'm afraid he's right, dear," Gram said.

"He may have been the one who hit Bernie," Rocky added. "We found blood and dog hairs in his trunk. Lab guys are checking it out now."

Jennie's mouth opened, but nothing came out. Something didn't fit, but Jennie couldn't think what. In fact, she couldn't think at all. "My brain is going numb."

"You need to rest," Mom said. "The doctor said you could probably go home this morning." She turned to Rocky. "I appreciate you trying to get to the bottom of this, but you're talking to Jennie as if she were working on the case. She isn't."

Jennie started to object, but Mom hushed her. "I know you like to think of yourself as a detective, but you're not. And until the police have Doug, or whoever is responsible, behind bars, you are staying at home. I don't intend to let you out of my sight until . . . well, until it's over." Mom gripped the bed rail and took a deep breath. "I may have lost one child, but God help me, I am not going to lose you."

You haven't lost Nick, Jennie wanted to argue, but didn't. She had no energy left for arguments she might not win.

If Jennie had ever thought of her mother as whimpy, she quickly altered her opinion. Susan McGrady was giving the orders now and everyone, including Gram, followed them. Mom wanted Jennie home. The doctor agreed. She didn't want Rocky or Gram talking to Jennie about the case. They promised not to say anything to Jennie without clearing it with her mother first.

Before leaving the hospital, Jennie stopped by to see Ryan. The T-shirt she'd wrapped around his head had been replaced by a gauzy white bandage. After greeting her, he tugged at her hand and pulled her forward for a kiss. "You know something, McGrady? You ought to wear some kind of a warning label."

"Huh?"

"Every time I'm around you I get hit on the head. You need a sign that says in big red letters: *Danger: being friends with me can be hazardous to your health.*"

"I'm sorry—"

"Hey, it isn't your fault. I'm okay. Really. The doctor just wants to keep me around until the swelling goes down. Maybe tomorrow."

Jennie squeezed his hand and told him about her mother's tirade. Instead of empathizing, he smiled. "It's about time somebody put a leash on you—ow!" he yelped when Jennie gave his shoulder a gentle punch.

At Mom's insistence, Jennie spent the rest of the day shuffling between her bed and the living room sofa. The arrangement didn't bother Jennie. At the moment, she ached too much to do anything but lie around.

Jennie's tolerance of her mother's overprotective attitude and her pain medication wore off at about the same time. It happened at ten the next morning when Jennie walked into the kitchen and overheard Mom on the phone.

"I'm sorry, Lisa, I'd rather you didn't."

Jennie reached for the phone. "Let me talk to her!"

Mom shook her head and held her hand up. Into the receiver she said, "Maybe tomorrow."

When Mom hung up and turned around, Jennie still had her mouth open. "I can't believe you just did that," she sputtered. "Why didn't you let me talk to her?"

"Because you need to rest. I didn't want her upsetting you."

"Upsetting me? You're the one who's upsetting me."

"Jennie, calm down. I said you could talk to her tomorrow." Mom brushed by her and headed for the stove. She removed the cover on what looked and smelled like chicken soup and stirred it.

"Mom, wanting to protect me from the bad guys is one thing, but Lisa's my cousin."

"She wanted to take you to the mall. I didn't think that was a good idea, okay?"

"No," Jennie whined. "It's not okay. You should have asked me."

"Asked you?" Mom spun around to face Jennie. "In case you've forgotten, I'm the parent around here. You, young lady, are the child."

"I am not a child. In case *you* haven't noticed, I'm sixteen. You told me I was old enough to make my own decisions. I thought you trusted me. Mom, you haven't screened my phone calls since I was . . . I can't remember when."

Mom glanced away, opened her mouth, then closed it again. Tears gathered in her eyes.

"I could understand if I'd done something wrong," Jennie went on, "but I haven't."

"Oh, Jennie, I'm so sorry. This whole thing is making me crazy. I feel like I'm losing control. I just don't want to lose you."

Jennie's anger dissipated like a balloon gone flat. "You're not going to lose me. Look, I promise not to do anything dangerous, okay?"

Mom covered the pot and sighed. "I guess it will have to do."

Gram came into the kitchen, poured herself a cup of coffee, and sat down at the table. "Susan, how well do you know Anne Stuart?"

"We've visited a few times. Apparently I don't know her as well as I thought. I never dreamed Chuck had been abusing her. Why do you ask?"

"I'd like you to invite Anne over here for a talk. I have a feeling she knows more about the children's disappearance than she's been letting on."

Mom sighed, "Apparently you don't agree with the police. You don't think Doug Reed is guilty?"

"He may be. Revenge is a strong motive. But somehow I doubt it. I suppose it's possible, but why on earth would he bring the dog back?"

"Maybe he wanted to make sure Bernie was found," Jennie suggested, setting her discussion with Mom aside.

"Exactly. That hardly sounds like the kind of cold-blooded person who would abduct three people, then bomb their car."

"I wondered about that. Doug may not be the brightest guy in the world, but I can't imagine him being dumb enough to steal a truck and run Ryan and me off the road."

Mom brushed aside a lock of auburn hair. "Are you saying you think Anne would be involved in those things? That's ludicrous."

"I agree. It's just that her actions seem a bit unusual. Anne didn't show up at the station yesterday to undergo questioning."

"Did she say why?" Jennie could understand Anne's reluctance; she hadn't wanted to go either.

"She was making funeral arrangements."

"Oh," Jennie felt sick. "Cathy's car." Jennie couldn't accept the possibility that Nick had died in that explosion. "You don't think Anne killed her sister and . . ." Jennie couldn't finish.

"No, dear." Gram placed her warm hand over Jennie's. "But she is jumping to conclusions. The forensics lab has found no evidence to suggest anyone was in the car. All they have so far are pieces of luggage and clothing."

"Then why would Anne be making funeral arrangements?"

"I think I can answer that," Mom said. "Maybe she wants it to be over. Sometimes it's easier to accept the fact that someone has died than to go on wondering where they are and what could have happened to them."

"Is that what you think, Mom?" Jennie asked, angered by her mother's logic. "You want Nick to be dead so you don't have to worry about it anymore?"

"Jennie! Of course not." Mom jerked to her feet and took her cup to the sink. "That's not what I meant." She turned back around, folding her arms across her chest. "I don't know what I meant. Part of me is ready to give up. Another part refuses. It's all very confusing."

Gram and Jennie agreed on that point. They also agreed that it was too soon to make funeral arrangements. "Do you really think talking to Anne will clear any of this up?" Mom asked.

Gram shrugged. "I don't know, but it's certainly worth a try."

While Mom called Anne, Jennie went to her room to call Lisa back.

"Jennie, I'm so glad you called. I have to talk to you."

"I take it you're feeling better. Mom said you were sick yesterday."

"I'm fine—just a flu bug, I guess. That's not important." Lisa chattered on the way she often did when she got nervous. "You don't believe Doug is guilty, do you? He isn't, you know. He told us . . ."

"What do you mean, he told you? Do you know where he is?"

"We have him hidden."

"You what?" Jennie sank onto her bed.

"It was B.J.'s idea, but we all went along with it. We thought if we could hide him out long enough the police would be able to find out who really ran you off the road and took Nick."

Jennie groaned. "Lisa, it doesn't work that way. Doug should never have run away. Now the police are convinced he did it. They're probably not even going to look for anyone else."

"But they have to!" Lisa gasped.

Jennie sank onto her bed. "No they don't. Besides, how do you know he's innocent? The police found blood in his car. He ran over Bernie."

"Not on purpose. He feels really bad about that. Bernie ran in front of his car. He was going to take him to the vet. Then he got scared when he found out Nick was missing. He was afraid the police would blame him."

"Of course they would. Did it ever occur to you they might be right?"

"Well, they're not."

Jennie groaned and ran a hand through her hair. "Look, Lisa, I know you guys want to help him, but you're making a mistake. The best way to help Doug is to tell him to turn himself in."

"I can't believe you'd say that. Maybe B.J. was right. She was afraid you'd blab to the cops. She didn't want me to tell you, but I thought you should know. You won't tell, will you?"

"Lisa, you're asking me to be an accomplice. It's against the law to harbor a criminal."

"Doug isn't a criminal—not anymore."

"You don't know that. He could be stringing you along."

"He's not. Please, Jennie, you've got to help him. I've talked to him. He wouldn't hurt you. Not in a million years. He didn't take Nick either."

Jennie pinched the bridge of her nose. Deep down she wanted to believe in Doug's innocence too. "Okay. I won't say anything for now—at least not until I talk to him. Look, I've got to go. Anne's downstairs. I'll talk to you later."

"I appreciate your having me over for coffee, Susan," Anne was saying as Jennie entered the kitchen. Gram and Mom sat at either side of her, and Jennie lowered herself into the chair next to Gram and opposite Anne. "The house seems so big and empty. I'd thought about going to stay with my parents, but the police want me to come in for questioning. Ironic, isn't it, that the police would want to spend so much time questioning the victims." Anne looked up from her coffee and offered Jennie a half-smile. "Hi, Jennie. I heard about your accident. Have the police found the young man who did it? It's hard to imagine having a criminal living so close right across the street."

"No." Jennie looked into Anne's wide pale-green eyes. "Personally, I think the police are after the wrong person."

"Really?" Anne broke eye contact with Jennie, glanced at Gram, then back at her coffee. She lifted the cup to her lips. "I thought they had proof."

"Proof doesn't always tell the entire story." Gram lifted her cup, but didn't take a drink. "How are you, Anne? It must be difficult for you, with Cathy and Hannah gone. And your husband . . . I understand he hasn't been home since Tuesday night. Jennie told us about the argument."

Anne lifted a delicate hand to her face. "N—no, he hasn't. We're getting a divorce."

"You haven't seen Chuck?" Jennie asked. "I thought maybe you'd gotten together. I saw your van at your parents' place. . . ."

She shook her head and frowned. "No. That must

have been someone else. I haven't been there. And I'm sure Chuck wouldn't have gone to see them on his own. He and Dad aren't on the best terms."

"Anne . . ." Gram scooted her chair closer to the table. "Did Cathy take the children?"

"Of course not. Why would you ask me that?"

"Did the police tell you about the man who saw Cathy leave?" Gram answered with another question.

"Yes. But he must have been wrong."

"He saw Cathy leave," Gram went on. "She was driving your Honda. He didn't see the children, but I suspect they were with her. Bernie was chasing the car and I doubt he'd have done that unless Nick was in it."

"I . . . I don't know," Anne stammered. "I suppose she may have taken them somewhere. Maybe to the park or to the store. I guess now we'll never know for sure." Anne set her cup down, drew a wad of tissues from her dress pocket, and dabbed at the tears gathering in her eyes. "I'm having the funeral tomorrow."

"Why?" Gram asked.

"What?" Anne raised her head up.

"The police haven't confirmed that Cathy or the kids were in the car when it exploded," Gram continued. "So why have you arranged for a funeral?"

"They were. They must have been. What other reason . . ." Anne drew in a ragged breath and raised her hands to cover her eyes.

Gram leaned forward, placing an arm across Anne's shoulder. "I think it's time to tell the truth, Anne. Tell us what really happened."

21

When Anne didn't answer, Gram kept talking. Jennie sat, mesmerized by her grandmother's skill in bringing Anne to the point of a confession. "We know Chuck was abusing you. Did he hurt Hannah too? Is that why you arranged for Cathy to take her and run? That is what happened, isn't it, Anne? While you and Chuck were gone, Cathy was supposed to take Hannah. That's why you had Cathy baby-sitting Hannah and not Jennie."

Anne nodded, tears streaming down her face. "It's true. Chuck said he'd never let me have custody of Hannah. He threatened to tell the police that I was abusing her. And he'd win. He can be very persuasive." Anne sucked in a shuddering breath and blew her nose.

"So you had to take her away from him?" Mom said in an empathetic tone.

"I didn't know what else to do. It seemed so easy at first. I confided in Cathy and she agreed to help me. We had it planned down to the last detail. She was supposed to abandon the car so everyone would think she and Hannah had been abducted. Mother was going to meet them at Mt. Hood Meadows to throw everyone off, and then take them to the beach. Mom and Dad have this property on the other side of the highway from the Bed and Breakfast. We were going to stay there for a few days, then go to Canada."

"So your parents knew all along?" Jennie asked.

"Only my mother. Dad would never go along with something like that. Mother knew what it was like to live with an abuser. Dad treated her like dirt. Oh, he never beat her up—he saved that for Cathy and me."

Gram shook her head. "Did you realize that by abducting Hannah and going into Canada, you would be committing a federal offense? You may have wanted to protect Hannah, but did you stop to consider what would happen to her with her mother in prison?"

"I knew we would be breaking the law, but—" Anne took another deep breath and pressed her hands to her forehead. "All I could think about was getting her away from Chuck. As long as he was only hitting me, I could live with it, but he'd started abusing Hannah. I couldn't let him do that."

In a voice much more controlled than Jennie felt, she asked Anne about Nick.

"Nick was never part of the plan. I don't know what happened to him. I don't know what happened to any of them." Anne dissolved in another barrage of tears.

"You don't know where they are?" Gram set her cup down with a clunk, sloshing coffee over the side. She didn't bother to mop it up.

"I . . . I know it sounds crazy. But you have to believe me. I haven't heard from my sister. She was supposed to call me when I got home. Like I said before, we'd arrange to have Mother pick her and Hannah up at Mt. Hood Meadows. Cathy was to abandon the car there. We thought it would throw everyone off our trail. Mother went to pick them up, but they never got there."

"And you have no idea what happened or what went wrong?"

"No. I . . . m-maybe it was Chuck, or that boy."

"You should have told the police," Gram said.

"I couldn't. I was about to commit a crime. Besides, I kept hoping I'd hear from Cathy." Anne began sobbing again.

Gram went to the phone. "You have to tell them, Anne. I'm going to call, let know we're coming. I'll drive you down to the station. You'll want a lawyer."

Anne nodded. "You're right. I'll tell them all I know. I just hope I'm not too late."

Around noon, when Ryan's doctor discharged him from the hospital, Jennie borrowed her mother's car to pick him up. Her Mustang had been totalled, and until the insurance company could work out a settlement she'd be carless.

Ryan's mom had intended to take him home, but Ryan managed to talk her into letting him stay at Jennie's until they found Nick.

Ryan still wore a bandage on his head, but it didn't cover the huge purple-green bruise that extended from the side of his head to his nose. On the way home she told him about Anne's confession.

"Whew," he whistled. "That's some story. You think her husband did it?"

"It's possible. No one seems to know where he is.

What I can't figure out, though, is why he'd run us off the road."

"Maybe Doug did that. Rocky seemed pretty sure."

"Not according to Lisa, B.J., Allison, and Jerry." Jennie told him about Lisa's phone call.

"This keeps getting better and better." Ryan put a hand up to shield his eyes from the sun. "Maybe we should talk to Doug—hear his side of the story."

Instead of heading home, Jennie called Lisa and arranged to pick her up on the way to visit Doug. In only a few minutes they were driving toward Trinity Center.

"I can't believe you have him hidden in the church." Jennie glanced in the rearview mirror at her redheaded cousin.

Lisa shrugged. "Well, it's not in the church, exactly. He's in the basement of the school—in the furnace room."

During the rest of the ten-minute trip, Jennie filled Lisa in on the latest details of the case. When they arrived at the church, Jerry opened a side door that led into a hallway separating the church from the high school. Jennie knew the layout of the building well. Her family had been going to church and school there ever since she could remember.

Several minutes later they descended the stairs past the "No admittance" sign and entered the furnace room. B.J., Doug, and Allison had already formed a semicircle on an old carpet remnant. Jennie sat opposite Doug, with Ryan to her left and Lisa to her right. She introduced Doug, B.J., Allison, and Jerry to Ryan.

"Thanks for not turning me in," Doug said. "I know it was stupid to run, but the cops will never believe the truth. I hardly believe it myself." Doug had a different look about him. The arrogance and hostility she'd seen in him earlier had been replaced with, what—humility? Sincerity?

"Tell me about Bernie."

"That was an accident. He ran right in front of me. I wanted to take him to the vet, but I was scared. Bernie was still alive and everything. Okay, it was stupid. I brought the dog home and then went to Hammond's. I really needed that job. I was going to tell you—until you came over and practically accused me of snatching Nick. Believe me, Jennie, I had nothing to do with Nick's disappearance."

"Why couldn't you have admitted you did it? Why did you run?"

"I saw the news, Jennie. When they reported the stuff about some woman seeing a guy at the park where they found Nick's shirt, I panicked. I knew it would only be a matter of time before they arrested me. I didn't know what to do until I talked to B.J." He gave B.J. a grateful look. Glancing back at Jennie he added, "I was pretty upset with you, McGrady—especially for calling the cops the night I locked myself out of the house. But I'd never hurt you."

B.J. slipped an arm through his. "I picked him up and brought him home and asked Allison and Jerry to help. Jerry had a key to the church."

"So, do you guys believe me?"

"I do," Ryan said.

Jennie gave Ryan an incredulous look. How could Ryan give in so easily? Doug seemed sincere enough, but Jennie wasn't convinced. Still, something in Doug's demeanor and his soft brown eyes made her waver. "I'd like to." *He has a record, McGrady,* she re-

169

minded herself. *He's a con artist. Yes,* another voice debated, *but people change and he has definitely changed.* "You seem different," she said.

Doug flashed her a shy grin. "Yeah, well, these guys have been trying to convert me. I've been reading books from the church library. At night I've been going up to the sanctuary—talking to God and that kind of stuff. Guess it's rubbing off."

Unfortunately, his change of heart had occurred *after* the attempt on her life. Besides, being a believer didn't clear him. "That's great, Doug," she said, deciding to affirm his decision on the chance he really had changed.

Jennie untangled her legs from the lotus position in which she'd been sitting and stood. "We'd better go, Johnson. I'm anxious to find out what the police thought about Anne's confession."

"Anne confessed?" B.J. and Allison asked together. "Why didn't you tell us?"

"I told Lisa on the way over. She can fill you in."

"Hey, McGrady." B.J. scrambled to her feet. "You won't narc on Doug, will you?"

"I can't promise anything like that, B.J." Jennie shifted her gaze to Doug. "You should turn yourself in. If you really have changed, it seems to me you'd want to do the right thing. Talk to Rocky. You can trust him to make sure you get a fair shake." Jennie turned and walked out; Ryan followed.

By the time Jennie and Ryan got back to the house, Mom had started dinner. Ryan collapsed on the couch. Jennie felt terrible. The guy had just come out of the hospital after suffering a concussion and she'd dragged him all over town. "Can I get you anything? Pain pills, an ice pack?"

"Yeah—both. Thanks."

After supplying Ryan with painkillers and a cold pack, Jennie joined her mother in the kitchen. "How did everything go with Anne?" She leaned over the counter and grabbed a carrot stick from the vegetable tray Mom was fixing.

"That poor woman. She's at home now—resting." Mom sliced the end off a stalk of celery. "She's been through so much. After interrogating her for two hours, the police have issued a warrant for Chuck." Mom set the knife down. "Would you finish this for me while I check the chicken?"

"Sure." Jennie took her mother's place at the counter and began slicing celery. "Do they think Chuck intercepted Anne's plan like she said?"

"Apparently, only they've added a twist. Remember Judson, Cathy's boyfriend?" Mom pulled a glass baking dish full of marinating chicken out of the fridge and began turning the pieces over.

Jennie nodded. "Is he still a suspect?"

"I don't think so. Apparently, he said something to the police about Cathy and . . . well, to make a long story short, they think Cathy and Chuck have been involved. Cathy may have told Chuck about Anne's plans."

"Chuck and Cathy? Mom, that's terrible." Jennie slashed through a wide stalk of celery. "I don't get it. This creep beats his wife. He's an unfaithful louse and Cathy finds him appealing? No way."

"I'm having a hard time understanding the logic myself. But Cathy does have a history of being attracted to abusive men. And you have to admit, until a few days ago, we saw Chuck as a very nice person."

"I guess it makes sense in a revolting sort of way. Anne confides her plan to Cathy. Cathy tells Chuck. She goes ahead with her plans to abduct Hannah, only instead of meeting Anne, she meets Chuck."

Then what, McGrady? Did they see you as a threat? Did they steal a truck and run you and Ryan off the road? The theory had possibilities. Still, it did little to resolve the most important question of all. What had they done with Nick? Jennie realized that no matter how terrifying the answer, she had to know.

Unfortunately, Mom was not the person to ask. "Where's Gram?"

"Resting. She talked to the forensics people today. They're certain that no one was in the car when it exploded. That's why the police think Chuck and Cathy may be in on it together. Now all they have to do is find them."

"Anne said something about going to Canada. Do you think they might have gone up there?"

"It's anyone's guess, Jennie. To be honest, I really don't care where they went. I just want my son back." Tears gathered in Mom's eyes and she brushed them away with the back of her hands.

Jennie set the knife aside and wrapped an arm around her mother's shoulders. "They'll find him, Mom. I know they will." *You don't know anything of the kind, McGrady.* Jennie tuned out the negative voice.

22

Mom finished turning the chicken, placed the dish back in the refrigerator, and washed her hands. "How would you feel about inviting Anne to eat with us tonight?" Mom paused to dry her hands. "I have a feeling she could use the company."

"I'm not sure I like the idea. I know Chuck abused her, but she shouldn't have tried to take Hannah. She should have gone to someone for help. The church would have found a safe place for her. There are women's shelters."

"It's hard to understand why people make the choices they do. Anne may have felt trapped and powerless. We mustn't judge her too harshly. I can't imagine what it would be like to have an abusive husband."

Jennie couldn't either. The one thing that puzzled her most of all was that Anne would let it go on so long. "Why didn't she just leave when it started?"

"It's difficult to say. Maybe she thought it was her fault. Sometimes when people abuse others, the victims end up feeling like they've done something wrong. That if they acted differently, the abuse wouldn't be happening. Maybe she was afraid? I've seen a number of television programs about battered women who stayed because they were terrified of what their husbands might do to them."

Jennie set the celery she'd cut up on the tray between the broccoli and the cauliflower. "I guess inviting her over would be a good idea."

The phone rang as Jennie reached for the doorknob. She grabbed for the receiver instead.

Her favorite policeman's mellow voice greeted her, then said, "Just wanted to thank you for getting Doug to turn himself in. The kid's okay. We took his statement and I'm pretty sure he'll be released."

"That's great. He was so afraid you wouldn't believe him."

"Well, he's not out of the woods yet. After getting Anne Stuart's statement this morning, we're looking at other options."

"Mom told me about Chuck and Cathy. You really think they were in on it together?"

"It's looking more and more that way. The deputy in Lincoln City says Mr. Williams reported his truck stolen last evening just after you and Ryan had been there. He accused Ryan until he found out Ryan was in the car with you. The truck turned up the next morning."

"Was it the one that hit us?"

"Hard to say. It was so pretty banged up to begin with. You said you saw the Stuarts' van in the Williams' parking lot?"

"Yes. I thought maybe Anne and Chuck were there, but I suppose he could have been there with Cathy— or, it may not have been their van at all. I mean, why would they go to the Williams'? Mr. and Mrs. Williams would never condone their actions. And why would they want me out of the way?"

"You were asking a lot of questions, both at Pacific University and at the Bed and Breakfast. It's entirely possible that one or both of them felt threatened. Look, Jennie," Rocky sounded annoyed. "I didn't call to get your opinion or to go over the case with you. I don't even want you to think about what might have happened. Leave that to us. I called to thank you for getting Doug to come in and—" His annoyance changed to concern. "And to tell you to be careful. Someone tried to kill you once. If they still see you as a threat they might try it again."

After hanging up, Jennie briefed her mother on Rocky's call, leaving out the part about her still being in danger. Mom didn't need any more worries. Besides, Jennie had no intention of investigating anything—at least not until after dinner.

As Jennie trudged across the lawns to invite Anne Stuart to dinner, she vacillated between feeling sorry for the woman and being angry with her. Anne may have thought running away was the best answer, but it wasn't. Jennie tried to imagine what it must have been like for Anne, living with a such a dark secret, trying to put on a front for people.

She ambled up the back steps, suddenly nervous. *Come on, McGrady,* she gave herself a pep talk. *Anne needs your support.* Jennie rang the doorbell. When Anne didn't answer, Jennie started to leave, then turned back. According to Mom, Anne was home. So why wasn't she answering the door?

Jennie could think of a lot of reasons. She might be hurt. Chuck and Cathy may have come back to finish her off. Or she may have decided to commit suicide. The possibilities propelled Jennie up the back porch steps. She rang the bell again. When no one answered, she tried the knob. It opened easily and Jennie stepped inside. She listened for sounds that might indicate someone was home, heard only the thumping of her heart in her ears. "Anne?" Jennie checked the laundry and living room. She swallowed hard, took a deep breath, and started up the stairs. "Anne!" Jennie called as she climbed the stairway.

"I'm in the bedroom, Jennie." Anne's voice held a hostile tone. Anne may not have answered the door because she didn't want to be bothered.

"I . . . I'm sorry." Jennie walked into the master bedroom. "When you didn't answer the door, I got worried."

A suitcase lay open on the bed along with a dozen or so articles of clothing. "You didn't need to worry. I'm fine." Anne's voice came from the walk-in closet.

"Are you going to stay with your parents?" Something about the picture didn't look or feel right. Anne was packing her things. Jennie could see Chuck's closet from her vantage point near the bed. It looked much as it had the day she and Lisa had searched the house. If Chuck had disappeared with Cathy, wouldn't he have taken his clothes?

"Yes." Anne exited the closet and dropped her armload of blouses on the bed, then went back for more. "Sorry I can't chat with you."

Jennie ignored the hint. "Mom wanted me to invite you for dinner," she said, wandering over to a dresser where Anne kept a collection of photos. They looked like such a normal family. Someone had propped a note next to Anne and Chuck's wedding picture. Jennie hadn't intended to read it. But the words jumped out at her.

I can no longer live with what I have become. I murdered Cathy and plan to kill Anne and Hannah, then kill myself. Chuck Stuart

Jennie pressed her hand to her mouth and backed away. "You just couldn't leave it alone, could you?" Anne emerged from the closet and threw several pairs of shoes on the floor.

Jennie tore her gaze from the letter and focused on Anne—or rather on the gun Anne retrieved from her suitcase. "I knew you'd be trouble from the start. I thought maybe running you off the road would get you out of the way, but no."

"You—" Jennie gasped. "You were behind this from the beginning? Then Chuck didn't find out about your plan. He wasn't having an affair with Cathy."

"Chuck and Cathy? That's rich." Anne's lips separated into what might have been a smile if there hadn't been so much hatred in her eyes. "Chuck didn't know until I told him."

"I don't understand. The note . . ."

"Chuck is only getting what he deserves. The police will eventually find his body. They'll have already read his confession and the case will be closed. Of course they'll never find our bodies, but after a while they'll stop looking."

"Did you kill him?"

Anne moved away from the bed, waving the gun from Jennie to the bed and back again. "Get over here and finish packing my things." She glanced at her watch. "Hurry."

Jennie stuffed the clothes into the oversized bag and zipped it shut. "You're not going to get away with this."

"Oh, but I am and you're going to help me."

"And if I don't?"

"Jennie, we have Nick."

The words slammed into Jennie's brain so hard she felt their impact clear down in her stomach. "Nick's shirt. The anonymous phone call about seeing a man in the park with Nick. That was you?"

"I wanted everyone to believe someone had abducted Cathy and the children. Don't worry, Nick is alive." Anne answered the question before Jennie could ask it. "But if you ever want to see him again, you'll do as I say. Understood?"

Jennie nodded. "What about the shirt? The police found blood on it."

"Hannah has one just like it. I cut myself and smeared blood all over it, and tossed it in some bushes." She glanced at her watch again. "Let's go. Take the bags downstairs."

Jennie picked them up. If the bags had been a little lighter and Anne a little closer, Jennie could have used them as weapons. *Even if you could overpower her, McGrady, would you want to? She's going to take you to Nick. The only chance you may have of finding him is to play along.*

Anne opened the garage door. The blue van was sitting inside. "Put the cases in the van."

Jennie set the cases just inside the door and slid them back beside a heavy canvas tarp.

"Now, get down on the floor. Face down. Put your hands behind you."

Anne tied Jennie's hands together, gagged her, then wrapped a piece of rope around Jennie's ankles. "That should hold you."

"Hmmm," Jennie protested, but her captor's only response was to slam the door shut. After a few minutes, Anne climbed in the driver's side, started the car, waited for the garage door opener to complete its grinding chore, then backed out.

"Cheer up, Jennie," Anne said after she'd gone a few blocks. "It's all for a good cause. We really didn't mean to take Nick. Truth is, Cathy sent him home. Only he wouldn't go. Hannah had told him she was frightened and begged him to come with her. I guess he wanted to protect her. Anyway, he climbed into the car when Cathy wasn't looking. She didn't know he was there until she met Mother at Timberline. By then the police were looking for him.

"Mother wanted to bring him back, but we couldn't take the chance. He knew too much." Anne hesitated, then in a lighter tone added, "We were going to call you when we'd gotten to Canada—to let you know where he was. Now I'm not sure what to do."

Jennie didn't know whether to cry or scream. They were all crazy. Apparently Anne felt she'd explained enough or maybe too much. Jennie shifted into what she hoped would be a more comfortable position. When she did, her foot caught on the tarp lying next to her. The tarp slid away from what it had been covering—Chuck Stuart's body.

23

Chuck's chalky white face lay less than a foot from hers. Jennie tried to scream. She looked away and tried to scoot back, but the seat blocked her.

"What's wrong?" Anne asked. "Oh, I see you've found him. Don't worry, he's not dead—yet. He came back and threatened to kill me if I didn't tell him where Cathy had taken the kids. I shot him. I'd gotten a gun for protection several months ago. I never meant to hurt him, but I couldn't let him ruin everything.

"I managed to stop the bleeding," Anne went on. "He'll be all right until I can decide where to stage his suicide."

Jennie whimpered. *Oh, God. She's totally lost her mind. What am I going to do? You've got to calm down, McGrady. Don't let her get to you.* Jennie willed her heart to slow down and concentrated on taking long deep breaths. She turned her head and looked at Chuck again, pushing the tarp farther down with her foot. His hands and feet were tied. Dried blood stains covered his left shoulder. Was he still alive? Jennie told herself she didn't care. Chuck Stuart's abusive behavior had started all this. He deserved to die.

No, a part of her argued. *What Chuck Stuart deserves is a long jail sentence. Not death.* Gritting her teeth she moved closer to Chuck and put her ear to his chest. Jennie could barely discern a heartbeat. His breathing was shallow and sporadic. He needed medical attention soon or he wouldn't make it to his own suicide.

What was Anne thinking? With a bullet wound like this in his shoulder, the police would never believe he'd killed himself. *That doesn't matter, now, McGrady,* she reminded herself. *What matters is getting to Nick and Hannah.* Then she'd find a way to deal with Anne and the others.

By the time Anne stopped the van, Jennie's earlier fears had taken a backseat to the pain in her body. She still hadn't recovered from the injuries she'd gotten when she fell out of her treed car. Anne opened the van door and helped Jennie out.

The air felt cool and moist against her skin. Sea gulls circled over head—they were at the beach. Anne closed the van's sliding door behind Jennie and untied her feet. "The cottage is this way, through the woods. My sister and I used to play in it when we were growing up. We'd hide out here when our father would go on his rampages. It was our refuge. Originally my parents planned to tear it down and build condominiums, but never did. Lucky for us."

The path cut through a stand of fir trees for about a hundred feet, then opened to a meadow. The cottage was tiny and old, probably built during the same era of the Bed & Breakfast, only this one hadn't been restored. Ann opened the door and motioned Jennie inside. It smelled musty and damp.

"Mommy, Mommy!" Hannah ran toward them

and wrapped her arms around Anne's legs. "Cathy be'd mean to Nick and he runned away."

"You let him go?"

Relief bubbled up inside Jennie. Nick had escaped. Only now what? Would he go for help? Would he be able to get away? *Go, Nick, run as fast as you can. Call Mom—you know the number.*

"I had the door locked. I was only out of the room for a minute . . ."

"How long ago?"

"About ten minutes. I wouldn't worry about it. The only place around other than the park is the Bed and Breakfast. If he makes it that far, Mother will bring him back here." Cathy frowned at Jennie and lifted her straight dishwater-blond bangs off her forehead. "What's she doing here?"

Anne extricated herself from Hannah. "She came in the house while I was packing. Saw the note." She glanced from Jennie to Hannah, then led Jennie toward a wooden chair that had at one time been painted white. Most of the paint had worn off. She handed Cathy the gun. "Do you think you can watch her?"

Jennie crossed her legs at the ankle and tucked her feet under the chair, hoping Anne wouldn't remember to tie them together again.

Anne picked Hannah up and walked toward what must have been a bedroom. "Hannah . . . honey, Mommy and Aunt Cathy have to talk. You stay in here for a few minutes and play, okay? We'll find Nick and go bye-bye again."

"Can Jennie come with us? I want her to baby-sit me. She's nice."

"We'll see. Now you play quietly. I'll come back in a few minutes."

"We can't take her with us," Cathy said as Anne approached them. "I don't like this. It seemed so easy when we started out. I never thought anyone would get hurt."

"I know. It's the last thing I wanted too. But we can't stop now. If the police find out what we've done, they'll take Hannah away from me for good. I couldn't bear that." Anne rubbed her forehead. "It'll still work out. Once we've gotten Hannah safely away, we can call someone and let them know where Jennie and Nick are."

Cathy heaved an exasperated sigh. "That might have worked for Nick, but Jennie's too dangerous. She knows too much."

"You're right. Well, I suppose we could kill her and blame that on Chuck too."

"How?"

"Look, right now the police are after you and Chuck. They know you didn't die in the car explosion. Maybe you and Chuck could die together in a fire—here in the house. Only it wouldn't be you, it would be Jennie. There'd definitely be two bodies." Anne turned to Jennie. "I really feel bad about this, you know. But you shouldn't have interfered."

Jennie stared at them. She'd never heard anyone discuss murder so calmly.

"We don't have time," Cathy argued. "Let's just go. We'll leave Jennie and Chuck here. No one ever comes to this place. It will be years before they find their bodies."

As the psycho sisters discussed Jennie's future—or

lack of one—Jennie looked around for a means of escape. The house had no phone. Her gaze passed over the small living room and caught a movement at the large picture window. A small head appeared above the windowsill. His dark blue eyes widened when he saw Jennie. Nick. *What if they see him?* She glanced back at her captors who were still trying to decide what to do. When she looked back, Nick was gone. Jennie had no idea what to do. Why had he come back?

"What was that?" Cathy held a hand up to silence Anne.

"I didn't hear anything."

"Someone's out there." Cathy peered out the small window in the back door. Jennie held her breath.

"I don't see anything." Cathy opened the door and stepped outside.

Jennie took advantage of the open door and charged through it. She tore past Cathy and ran in the opposite direction from where she'd seen Nick. *God, please keep him safe,* she prayed as she sprinted across the clearing into the woods. She glanced back. Both women were chasing her. Good. That would give Nick a chance to get away. Maybe she could get to the road—or the park. There'll be a pay phone in the park.

Jennie stumbled over an exposed root. She managed to right herself and avoid plunging headlong into the dirt, but only for a few seconds. Anne's tackle knocked her to the ground.

They dragged Jennie back into the house and dumped her onto the chair. "I told you she was trouble," Cathy panted.

"You were supposed to watch her. Where's the gun?"

Cathy pointed to the kitchen table. "It was lying right here."

"Oh no." Anne's gaze traveled to the open door leading into the bedroom. "Hannah!" Anne raced toward the room, stopped at the door, and turned around. "She's not here," she gasped. "I've got to find her. Tie Jennie to the chair and make sure she can't walk. We'll deal with her later."

Anne ran out the door and Cathy jerked Jennie backward, then knelt down to wrap the cord around Jennie's legs.

"You let my sister go 'for I shoot you." Nick was standing in the doorway of the bedroom. Hannah beside him. He had the gun pointed straight at them. "Put that thing down," Cathy ordered, momentarily forgetting her task.

Acting on pure instinct, Jennie brought her knees to her chest, planted her feet against Cathy and pushed with all her might. Cathy yelped and fell backward, hitting her head on the corner of the coffee table near the couch. She went limp.

"Hmmm." Jennie wriggled her hands trying to loosen the knots. Nick lowered the gun and ran to her side.

"She was goin' to hurt you." He reached up and pulled the gag from Jennie's mouth. "We took the gun and hided under the bed."

Jennie didn't know whether to praise him or scold him. Kids and guns could be a lethal combination. She decided on praise—they could talk about the other later. "Good job, Nick. Now, put the gun on the floor and untie my hands. Hurry. Hannah's mommy will be back any minute."

Nick knelt behind her and worked at the knots. Within seconds he'd freed her.

Jennie scooped up the gun, checked the safety, and tucked it in her waistband at the small of her back. After dragging Cathy into the bedroom, Jennie dumped her onto the bed, tied her hands together, and secured her to the wooden bed post.

"You kids stay in the house," Jennie ordered as she closed the door to the bedroom. She started to leave, then stopped, dropped to her knees, and gathered Nick and Hannah into her arms and hugged them. "I'm so glad to see you two." Jennie held back the tears. "Listen, I have to go find Hannah's mommy. I'll come back as soon as I can." Jennie got to her feet, took a deep breath, and left.

"Hannah!" She heard Anne calling in the distance. Jennie ran toward the voice, following the trail they'd come in on. She slowed as she reached the clearing where Anne had parked the van. Anne stood at the edge of the long gravel driveway leading to the highway. She glanced around, then continued down the road. It hadn't taken much to overpower Cathy. The college student was small and wiry. Anne had a small build too, but she was much stronger.

Her best chance would be to take Anne by surprise. Jennie stepped into the clearing, then using the van as a shield, picked up a rock and threw it into the woods. Anne whipped around and jogged back toward the cars.

"Hannah, it's Mommy. Come on, sweetheart. It's time to go bye-bye."

When Anne passed the car, Jennie sprang from her hiding place, hitting Anne from behind. Anne grunted as she belly-flopped onto the hard, rocky ground. Jennie quickly straddled her and pulled Anne's hands back. "I've got the gun," she said in a voice that she hoped sounded tough and authoritative. "So I suggest you do what I say." She really did have a gun, but had no intention of using it.

"You have to let me go, Jennie. Please. I won't hurt you. I promise. Just let us take Hannah. You can have Nick." Anne's pleas turned to sobs. "Don't you understand? The state will give Chuck custody of my baby."

Jennie swallowed back the lump forming in her throat and shook her head. "I can't."

———

Jennie heard the sirens long before the crunch of gravel. Four cars from the Lincoln County Sheriff's department pulled into the small parking area. After a few tense moments of finding out who was who, Jennie told them what had happened. One deputy handcuffed Anne and helped her into the back of a patrol car. Another examined Chuck and radioed for an ambulance. Two of them, a man and a woman, ordered Jennie to stay put and headed for the house.

"How did you find us?" Jennie asked the deputy standing beside her. "How did you know where we were?"

"We received word from Portland around seven that you and Anne Stuart were missing. Mr. Williams called us a few minutes ago. Apparently his wife broke down after she heard about you and confessed the whole story." He shook his head. "Said she couldn't go along with it anymore. Her girls had just gone too far."

In less than five minutes, the officers emerged with Cathy in the lead. The male officer followed, then the woman, carrying Hannah and holding Nick's hand. Nick and Hannah squirmed away from Officer Larson's arms and attached themselves to Jennie's legs.

"Randall, Horrowitz," the deputy standing next to Jenny barked. "You two take the prisoners in. Larson," he said to the woman who'd brought Nick and Hannah out. "Get these kids to the hospital and notify the family." He hesitated, glanced down at Hannah, and in a softer voice added, "Better call Children Services for that one."

———

Three hours later, the glass doors of the hospital waiting room opened. Mom and Gram walked in. Nick flew off his chair and into Mom's arms. Mom hugged and kissed him, then reached for Jennie. Gram wrapped her arms around all of them.

When they finally separated, Mom was still holding Nick. "Hey, sweetheart." She kissed his cheek and hugged him again. "There's somebody waiting in the car who can't wait to see you."

Actually there were two somebodies. Bernie, who covered Nick in sloppy kisses, and Michael. Since Nick didn't want to let go of either of them, Mom settled him in the backseat between her and Michael, and let Bernie lay on their laps. Jennie wondered if Mom and Michael had worked things out, but didn't ask. She'd find out soon enough.

Jennie and Gram sat in front, with Gram as the designated driver. They were a block from the hospital when Nick yelled, "Gram! Stop! We gotta go back."

Gram braked and pulled over to a curb.

"Shhh," Mom soothed. "What's the matter?"

"Hannah!" Nick twisted around in his seat and looked out the back window. "We gotta go back and get her."

"Oh, honey, Hannah can't come with us."

"But she has to!" Nick cried. "She'll be scared."

24

Jennie heard them come in, but pretended to be asleep. "Shhh. We gotta be quiet," Nick whispered. "She gets real grumpy if you wake her up too early."

Jennie pulled the covers over her face to hide her smile.

"M-maybe we should go away." Hannah's voice held a note of fear, and that concerned Jennie whenever she heard it.

"It'll take time," Mom had said. Time to mend the wounds caused by an abusive father and a mother who'd made some tragic choices. Jennie, Nick, and Mom had unanimously agreed to make Hannah part of their family, and Mom had been granted temporary custody as a foster parent.

"It's okay," Nick reassured Hannah. "Come on. It's a good kind of grumpy 'cause she doesn't really mean it."

A large pink tongue assaulted Jennie's forehead. She sneaked a hand out from under the covers to pet Bernie's silky fur.

Jennie felt the bed shift as the kids climbed onto it. "Who's that climbing on my bed," Jennie asked in her deepest voice. They shrieked, then giggled as Jennie tossed back the covers and grabbed them.

The wrestling and giggles continued until Mom came in and pulled Nick and Hannah off Jennie. "You might want to get dressed. Ryan's downstairs waiting for you to take him to the airport."

This time it was Jennie's turn to shriek. She'd forgotten all about it. Which probably meant she didn't want to remember. She and Ryan had gone out on the big date he'd promised her, the night before. He'd brought her flowers and . . . *Not now, McGrady. You can think about that later. Right now you've got to move.*

Twenty minutes before his flight, Jennie dropped him off at the curb. "I'll miss you," she whispered in his ear when he hugged her.

"Me too." Ryan chuckled. "I mean—I won't miss me. I'll miss you." He released her and took a step back. "Hey, promise me you'll stay out of trouble while I'm gone."

Jennie laughed. "I'll try." She waved goodbye until he disappeared through the revolving door.

Stay out of trouble? He'd been teasing and serious at the same time. Jennie wondered what he'd have said if he'd known about the late night phone call—or the plea for help from the girl with the rainbow hair.

Jennie climbed into the car she'd gotten in the insurance settlement—another Mustang, only this one was new and fire-engine red. A wide grin spread across her face as she snapped the seat belt in place and drove away.

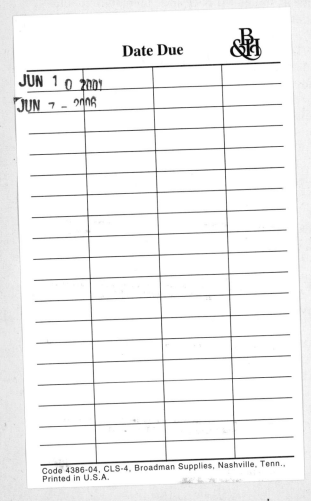